SEABIRD

The Gulf of Mexico is a marvellous setting for a film location and the Keys all around are wonderful grounds for Nick to go bird-watching. But there are other attractions too. When Nick and Jenny Rawson hear the legend of the ghostly Italian pirate who haunts the islands looking for his treasure, they go to investigate on a nearby Key. But once there, they stumble upon a secret plot. And the evil perpetrators have no intention at all of allowing them to spoil it.

About the Author

Keith Miles was born and brought up in Cardiff, and started writing plays and revues when at school there. For some months he lived in Yugoslavia before going to Oxford University to study history. His involvement in drama as an undergraduate was considerable. He had a play performed at the National Union of Students' drama festival and also toured with them as an actor, in Turkey.

After leaving Oxford, Keith lectured in history for three years in a college of further education in Wolverhampton. Since 1966 however, he has been a freelance writer. He has continued to work in every aspect of drama, including a spell as a drama lecturer in a maximum security prison, but in the last ten years, has concentrated on writing books – including adult fiction and non-fiction as well as children's fiction.

Seabird

Keith Miles

KNIGHT BOOKS
Hodder and Stoughton

To Elizabeth Roy for helping this particular seabird to fly

First published by Knight Books 1987
Second impression 1987

British Library C.I.P.

Miles, Keith
Seabird.—(Action scene; no. 2)
I. Title II. Series
823'.914[J] PZ78

ISBN 0-340-40438-8

The characters and situations in this book are entirely imaginary and bear no relation to any real person or actual happening.

Printed and bound in Great Britain for Hodder and Stoughton Paperbacks, a division of Hodder and Stoughton Ltd., Mill Road, Dunton Green, Sevenoaks, Kent TN13 2YA. (Editorial Office: 47 Bedford Square, London WC1B 3DP) by Richard Clay Ltd., Bungay, Suffolk

Prologue

The deck of the pirate ship was a mass of writhing bodies as the two crews struggled for mastery. Steel clashed with steel, pistols were fired at point-blank range, bare hands were used to punch and gouge and strangle. The noise was deafening and blood flowed freely.

It was truly a fight to the death.

Redbeard's men seemed to be winning at first, but the greater strength and determination of Captain Valdano's crew soon began to tell. Valdano himself – the Phantom Pirate – was at the centre of the action, holding off three enemy swords with his flashing cutlass and leading as ever by courageous example. It was only a matter of time before he gained control of the whole ship and rid the seas of his hated rival.

But the villainous Redbeard was not finished yet.

Seeing that he was now on the losing side, he tried one last desperate move. He hacked his way to his cabin where the beautiful Marie-Louise, the Governor's daughter, was locked up. The girl screamed in horror as the hideous face of Redbeard came around the door. She pushed him off but her resistance was in vain.

A giant of a man, Redbeard scooped her up with ease.

Back on deck, Valdano was fighting with all his usual skill and daring. A thrust with his cutlass disposed of yet another adversary and he looked for more work. The cry took his eyes upwards.

'Valdano!'

Redbeard was climbing the rigging of the mainmast with the hapless Marie-Louise under his arm. She let out a second yell.

'Valdano! Help me!'

The Phantom Pirate responded to the call at once.

Showing remarkable nimbleness, Redbeard scrambled higher and higher. The girl was held in a grip of iron. She had no hope of escape. Her captor went on until he reached the upper main topgallant sail. When he set Marie-Louise's feet down on the timber, she threw both arms around the mast and clung grimly to it.

Far below them, the slaughter continued.

Redbeard gave a deep laugh. He sensed that his plan would work. With the governor's daughter as his hostage, he might yet win. Valdano could beat him in a fair fight but the Phantom Pirate had one weakness.

He was in love with Marie-Louise.

Pulling a pistol from his belt, Redbeard aimed it at the ship's bell and discharged it. There was a loud clang. Everyone paused for an instant. A roar came down from the mainmast.

'Valdano!' warned Redbeard. 'Tell your men to throw down their weapons or I'll kill her!'

There was no movement on deck. The pirates froze where they were and gazed upwards. Redbeard's men started to grin in triumph. Valdano's crew were dismayed. Marie-Louise hung on to the mast as the vessel rolled in the swell.

Redbeard scoured the deck for his arch-enemy.

'Answer me, Valdano!' he ordered. 'Where *are* you?'

'Behind you!' came the reply.

The Phantom Pirate had ascended the mizen-mast until he was level with the others. Using a long rope, he was swinging through the air towards them. Redbeard turned around in time to take the full impact on his chest. He was knocked back against the sail, but he recovered at once to grapple with Valdano.

The fight on deck was over. Victory would be decided aloft.

Marie-Louise watched in terror as the pirate captains fought it out. Balancing precariously on the boom and urged on by their men, they wrestled violently with each other. Redbeard was much bigger and more powerful than his handsome opponent and the girl feared for Valdano's safety.

But the Phantom Pirate was equal to the challenge.

As Redbeard got a grip on him and began to force him slowly backwards, Valdano pretended to resist. Then, as the pressure on him increased, he suddenly jumped backwards and grabbed a rope that was dangling from a spar. Redbeard's immense weight was now used against himself. Instead of pushing Valdano off the boom, *he* was the one who was launched into space.

He let out a howl of anger as his huge body fell through the air. Then he hit the deck with a sickening thud and all around there was silence. His crew put down their weapons and surrendered. Valdano had won.

The agile captain swung himself back up on to the boom and stepped across to comfort Marie-Louise. Her life had been saved by the Phantom Pirate. She rewarded him with a kiss.

The film cameras stopped rolling and the cast relaxed.

Another action scene was over.

One

Distress Signal

Wearing a red bikini and a frown of concentration, Jenny Rawson stretched both arms out in front of her and raised herself up on her toes. When she was quite composed, she bent her legs at the knees, straightened them to thrust herself off the edge of the yacht, did a complete somersault then entered the water head first with a minimum of splash.

It was an excellent dive and Liza was impressed.

'She's good. She's very good.'

'Yes,' conceded Max Rawson. 'Jenny's coming along.'

'She's doing much more than that,' argued Liza. 'Your daughter is a first-rate swimmer and her diving gets better all the time. Jenny works hard at it. She obviously takes after you, Max.'

'That's what worries me.'

Max Rawson looked down at his daughter with a mixture of fondness and concern. He was very proud of Jenny's all-round sporting ability, but he was unhappy about her ambition to follow him into the stunt business. The young teenager was caught up in the glamour of the job whereas her father knew all the dangers and uncertainties involved.

The sea was a turquoise mirror that shone in the bright sunshine. Jenny did a leisurely breaststroke until she reached her brother, Nick, who was treading water some forty metres or so away. He was over a year older than her but he lacked her solid build and her flair as a swimmer.

She issued a challenge.

'Race you back!'

'I don't want to, Jenny.'

'You're scared of losing.'

'No, I'm not.'

'Come on then.'

'Jenny, I'm not racing you.'

'I'll give you five metres' start.'

'Leave me alone.'

'Ten.'

'Shove off, will you?'

'Fifteen.'

'No!'

'Cowardy custard!'

Nick responded to the jeer at once. Putting a hand on top of her head, he pushed her down under the water then began to swim back for all he was worth. But though his arms flailed bravely away and his legs kicked madly, he made slow progress. Nick had no real rhythm. He was all foam and no speed.

Jenny was in a different class. She surfaced,

spat out a mouthful of salt water, giggled aloud then set off in pursuit. Her crawl was much smoother and far more effective than anything her brother could manage and she soon overhauled him. While he was still threshing about wildly in the sea, she reached the yacht and climbed up the rope ladder. She felt pleased with herself.

When Nick finally joined her on deck, they towelled themselves off then went across to their father. Liza was still sitting at the table with Max and she was very complimentary.

'Well done, Jenny!'

'Thanks. I always beat Nick.'

'That's not true,' he protested.

'Me, Tarzan,' boasted his sister. 'Him, Jane.'

'Stop showing off, Jenny,' said Max firmly.

'Sorry.'

The children sat down and he poured them each a glass of iced orange juice. Nick sipped his drink but Jenny finished hers in one long, thirsty gulp.

Because their father was a famous stuntman, they usually spent their holidays on location with him. The exciting career of Max Rawson had taken them all around the globe and they revelled in their opportunities. It made them the envy of their schoolfriends back in England.

The film which had brought them out to the Gulf of Mexico was *The Phantom Pirate*, a stirring saga of a Robin Hood of the high seas who plundered the rich to help the poor. Max was playing the title role in the many action sequences. Since he was also stunt co-ordinator on the film, he was kept extremely busy and was glad that he had such an expert team under him.

Liza Davies was an important part of that team. Short, slim and lithe, she was an attractive woman in her twenties who had already built up a reputation for herself as a stuntwoman. She doubled for the actress playing the part of Marie-Louise, the Governor's daughter, and she was called upon to take a lot of risks infront of the camera.

Nick and Jenny had become close friends with her. Whenever the cast and film crew went back to the yacht that was their floating home, Liza always spent the time with Max and his children. She took a genuine interest in the two teenagers.

'How are you enjoying Florida?' she asked.

'It's fantastic!' replied Nick. 'The bird life is marvellous.'

'Yes, it must be a bird-watcher's dream.' Liza turned to Jenny. 'And what about you?'

'It's nice,' said the girl, dutifully. 'I like it.'

'You don't sound very enthusiastic.'

'Oh, I am,' returned Jenny. 'I love watching you and Daddy doing your stunts together. That bit is fab. It's just that…' She gave a shrug. 'Well, when I heard we were coming to Florida, I hoped it'd be to Miami.'

'Why there?'

'Her favourite telly series,' explained Nick.

'*Miami Vice.*'

'Always wanted to see what it was really like,' added Jenny.

'Big, brash and unbearably noisy,' said Max.

'You're much better off in Key West,' urged Liza. 'It's a lovely island with a fascinating history.'

'But it's not Miami,' sighed the girl. 'Besides, we never seem to *be* in Key West. We're usually stuck out in the middle of the sea like today. And it can get boring sometimes.'

'Not if you study birds,' reminded Nick.

'Well, I don't!'

'There are masses of other things to do,' suggested Liza. 'Sailing, swimming, diving, fishing, deck games.'

'It's still not Miami.'

Max Rawson smiled indulgently and patted her arm.

'Not to worry. When we've finished here, maybe we can grab a few days in Miami. Okay?'

Jenny leaned over to hug him and kissed him on the cheek.

'Daddy – you're wonderful!'

'As long as it cheers you up.'

'Oh, it does. I feel on top of the world now.'

She grabbed the jug and poured herself another glass of orange juice. After drinking it in one go, she beamed happily at them.

'When's lunch? I'm starving!'

The others laughed. Jenny was her old self again.

Ed Garrett stepped down into the boat to check that everything was in order. He was a tall, thin, wiry man with a tanned face that was half-covered by a grizzled white beard. In sleeveless vest, canvas trousers and peaked cap, he looked exactly what he was. A retired sailor with a lifetime's rich experience at sea.

The film company made good use of that experience. Ed Garrett was employed as a consultant on nautical matters. His knowledge of piracy, sailing ships, tides, weather and marine life was remarkable. Given in a throaty American drawl, his advice was always reliable.

His affable manner, sense of humour and fund of colourful stories made him a popular figure. Nick Rawson was particularly fond of him. Ed had been very helpful in a number of ways and he was now doing the boy a special favour.

'Can we come aboard, Ed?'

'Yes,' said the old man. 'You're all set?'

Nick lowered himself down into the craft and it bobbed in the water. Jenny followed him. They were off on a bird-watching trip in a small boat with an outboard motor. Though she had no interest in birds, Jenny was going along because there was no filming that afternoon and because she had been promised a turn at steering the boat.

Ed climbed back on to the yacht and leaned over the rail.

'Now take care. Do like I told you.'

We will,' agreed Nick. 'And thanks.'

'If you get lost, send me a postcard.'

'How can we do that?' asked Jenny.

She saw Ed's gap-toothed grin and realised that he was joking. Nick was holding a folded map in his hand. He waved it.

'According to this, there's a big cluster of islands directly north of here.'

'Stay away from them,' cautioned Ed.

'But one of them is a heron colony.'

'Sail due west and you'll find all the birds you want. Take my word for it. Go thataway.'

He pointed a bony finger towards the dark shapes on the horizon. Nick nodded, put the map aside and started the motor up. It roared into life. The children settled themselves down in the boat.

Ed loosened the rope that moored them to the yacht.

'What are you waiting for?' he yelled. 'Go get 'em!'

They shouted their farewells above the rasp of the motor then moved steadily out into open water. Leaving a white triangle of foam in their wake, they cruised on, past the three-masted pirate ship that was being used in the film.

It looked imposing and romantic against the blue sky but they knew that in reality it was covered with cables, cameras, sound and lighting equipment. There was also a huge wind machine standing on the poop deck so that the sails could billow to order.

Nick and Jenny forgot all about *The Phantom Pirate* as they glided across the surface of the water. The breeze was cool and refreshing and they had a tremendous sense of freedom. It was exhilarating. Nick let his sister take over the steering so that he could concentrate on the serious task of bird-watching.

They saw gulls, terns, herons, pelicans and a lone cormorant. Nick made a note of his sightings in a pad and described the plumage and behaviour of the individual birds. All the information would later be transferred to his beloved record book.

Time passed easily. Jenny's mind played with an idea.

'I wish we still had pirates today.'

'What?'

'Sailing the seven seas under the skull and crossbones. Must have been terrific fun. I'd have loved it.'

'They didn't have girl pirates, silly.'

'I'm not a girl,' she claimed. 'I'm a young woman.'

'Still don't see you with a beard and a patch over one eye.'

Nick continued to scan the surroundings through his binoculars while Jenny chatted on about the joys of the buccaneering life. Neither of them noticed that the boat had gone right off course. Instead of heading due west, it had veered off to the right and was now moving north.

Jenny's reverie was shattered by her brother.

'We *do* still have pirates today!'

'Where?'

'Over there. Look!'

She turned her head and saw what he meant. A gull was flying across the sea with a fish in its beak. A much larger bird descended from the sky and threatened it. When the food was dropped, the second bird swooped down and seized it before it hit the water.

It was an act of piracy in broad daylight.

'What on earth is it, Nick?'

'A frigate bird. Also called a man-of-war.'

'It's enormous.'

'They sometimes have a wing span of nearly eight metres.'

'Where is it going now?'

'Probably taking the food back to the nest. Living in a warm climate, they're able to breed all the year round.'

For once, Jenny was interested in a bird.

'Let's follow it.'

'We'll never keep up with it. The frigate bird is one of the most aerodynamic in the world. It will leave us standing.'

'Why did it steal that fish?'

'Because it's not very good at catching its own. They rarely settle on the water, because their feet are small and they have reduced webs. Also, their plumage gets soaked very easily because their oil glands are not efficient enough.'

'What does that mean?'

'It means that they have to spread their wings out to dry them before they can take off again. In other words they don't like getting wet, so they do a lot of their fishing in mid-air.'

All the time that he was talking, Nick kept his binoculars on the frigate bird. Although it was some distance away from them now, its destination was clear. It was losing height as it approached a group of small islands.

Jenny steered the boat after it as if they were involved in a chase. The frigate bird had intrigued her and she wanted to know more about it. She was delighted when they saw it coming in to land. The boat sputtered on until it was about fifty metres from the island, then Nick gave the order to stop the engine. They drifted slowly on the incoming tide and he fixed his lenses on a sight that he had never seen before.

'There's a whole colony of them!'

'Let me see!' she demanded, trying to grab the binoculars.

'Wait a minute.'

Nick ran his trained eye over the island. He saw dozens of frigate birds. Their nests were large, untidy structures of sticks and they seemed to have been sited in the most haphazard way. Some were on tall mangrove trees, others were on low bushes and a few were on the ground. Nick could have stayed there and observed it all for hours but he was distracted.

There was movement on the island next to the

colony.

When he swung his binoculars across, he caught a glimpse of a man, standing on a mound and waving a white shirt frantically in the air. As the bare-chested figure tried to attract his attention, Nick saw something glinting on the man's wrist.

'Quick, Jenny!' he said, handing her the glasses.

'What am I supposed to look at?'

'That island over there. There's a man waving to us.'

'Is there?'

Jenny focussed the binoculars but she could see no man.

'Are you sure you weren't making it up, Nick?'

'Of course I am.'

'There's nobody there now.'

'There was, Jenny. I'm certain of it.'

Nick Rawson was certain of something else as well.

What he had seen was a distress signal.

Two

The Phantom Pirate

They took it in turns to search the island through the binoculars. There was no sign of life. The place was utterly deserted. Jenny teased her brother and told him he was hallucinating but he was convinced that he had not been mistaken.

Someone needed help.

'Let's take a closer look,' he decided.

'I'll do it,' she volunteered, reaching for the pull-start. With a sudden jerk, she got the motor going first time. 'How was that?'

'Perfect. Now take me slowly round that island.'

'Aye, aye, sir.'

Jenny gave a mock salute then obeyed orders. Steering the boat carefully through the shallow water, she went in a circle around the island. Like all the other Keys in that cluster, it was low, flat, shapeless and covered in trees and bushes. It took them less than five minutes to complete a circuit around the perimeter. Nick studied the island carefully through his glasses but he saw nobody.

'Satisfied now?' asked his sister.

'No. I want to go ashore.'

'What for?'

'That was a distress signal. We've got to answer it.'

'I think it was sunstroke. You're seeing things.'

'Steer us in.'

'But I don't *want* to go ashore, Nick.'

'You don't have to. I'll manage on my own, thanks.'

'It's a waste of time.'

'Take me in to that beach.'

'I think we should go back now,' said Jenny. 'We've come miles out of our way as it is.'

'What do you mean?'

'See for yourself.' She indicated the compass that Ed Garrett had considerately loaned them. 'We went right off course somehow. These islands are due north of the yacht.'

Nick was somewhat taken aback by the news. He used his binoculars to comb the sea behind them. Their yacht, the *Florida Star*, was not even a friendly speck on the horizon. It was disturbing.

'We ought to head straight back,' asserted Jenny.

'Not until I've been ashore.'

'There's nobody there.'

'Then who was it I saw?'

'Probably a large bird, flapping its wings.'

'Can you imagine *me* making a mistake about a bird?' he argued. 'It was a man alright. Waving a shirt. Summoning help.'

'Then where is he now?'

'That's what I hope to find out.'

Before Jenny could protest, he took over the steering and eased the boat towards the shore. When they got close to the beach, he killed the motor, then swung it up out of the water on its hinge so that there was no danger of the propeller getting caught in the sand.

'Make it quick!' ordered Jenny.

'Two minutes. That's all I ask.'

'That's all you'll get.'

Nick jumped over the side of the boat into a metre of water and ran ashore. The boat drifted on until its nose met dry sand. Jenny hopped out and used the rope to pull it away from the lick of the waves. She glanced at her watch. Fifteen seconds had gone by already.

Her brother knew exactly where he was going. Sprinting along the beach, he reached an outcrop of rock that formed the highest point on the island. When he had clambered to the top, he commanded an excellent view. The binoculars came into use again but he saw no bare-chested man through them.

The island seemed to be completely uninhabited.

Nick cupped his hands to form a megaphone.

'Is anybody there?' he shouted.

There was a long silence, broken only by the cry of some birds wheeling overhead. Nick took a deep breath and gave a louder yell.

'Hello! Can you hear me!'

'Yes!' shrieked Jenny from the shoreline. 'And your two minutes is up, Nick Rawson!'

He took one more look through his glasses, then heaved a sigh of resignation. The man had vanished into thin air. Though his instinct was to make a thorough search, he decided that it was perhaps time to head back. Jenny re-inforced that decision.

'I'm going without you!'

She was pushing the boat back into the water. He scrambled down the rocks and raced across the sand. Jenny was fixing the outboard motor back in position when he waded out to her.

'I told you it would be a wild goose chase,' she observed.

'There's somebody on that island,' he insisted.

'Yes - The Invisible Man. Now get in.'

Nick hauled himself into the boat and his sister started the motor up. As they moved away from the island, he glanced back but there was still nobody to be seen. It was quite bewildering.

'Wonder what's on the menu for tea,' mused Jenny.

But her brother did not even hear her. He was too preoccupied. While she was thinking about the next meal, he was puzzling over what had happened. Doubts began to crowd in on him. Did he *really* see someone waving a shirt? Or had his sharp eyes deceived him this time?

Nick Rawson scratched his head. He was mystified.

Back on the island, there was movement among the trees. A short, tubby man in a crumpled white suit put his swarthy face around the trunk of a palm. He stared after the receding boat then he raised a hand to wipe the perspiration from his brow. His black, pencil-thin moustache twitched in irritation.

Lying on the ground beside him, was a figure dressed only in trousers and sandals. He was bound and gagged. A shirt was hidden under a bush nearby.

The fat man used a toe to turn his companion over so that the latter was on his back. He glared down at his prisoner who was a lean, grey-haired man with an air of distinction about him. The captor spoke with a heavy accent.

'That was very stupid. You pay for it. Bad.'

He turned to look once more after the boat.

The trouble with stunts was that they took an enormous amount of time to set up. Action scenes lasting a few minutes might need hours of preparation. As co-ordinator, Max Rawson was involved in all the preparation. While his team spent the afternoon resting, he worked with the director and technicians to make all the necessary alterations on the sailing ship. By early evening, they were ready.

Captain Valdano had to defeat Redbeard once more.

The evil pirate had not in fact plummeted to his death from a great height. His fall had been real enough but he had made a soft landing. Instead of smashing into the deck, he had been caught obligingly in a safety net. Shooting from below, however, a camera had filmed his fall in such a way as to make it look completely authentic.

The incident now had to be shot from above and so a camera had to be hoisted up the mainmast and fixed in position. When Redbeard was thrown off the boom, he would now be seen hurtling down towards the solid timber of the deck. Except that this timber was not solid.

It was an optical illusion.

When the safety net was removed, another way of breaking the fall had to be used. Planking was lifted from the deck to reveal a deep hold that was filled with scores of empty cardboard boxes. False planking made out of balsa wood was put over the hold. From above, the deck looked quite realistic.

As he dropped down through the air, the stuntman taking the role of Redbeard would hit the balsa wood, go straight through it, then land on the cardboard boxes. The camera would film the whole sequence but it would later be edited so that an audience would only see it up to the split second that he made contact with the deck.

It was a fairly straightforward stunt, but Max

Rawson was a perfectionist. Before he asked Redbeard to rehearse the fall, he had a trial run-through himself. Hurling himself from high up on the mainmast, he went through the balsa wood as if it were paper and then felt the empty boxes concertina beneath him.

The stunt worked. It was effective and safe.

Everyone now got back into costume and the principals took their places aloft. Marie-Louise watched in terror again as the pirate captains went into their fight routine. After a long struggle, Redbeard was thrown from on high. He fell like a stone before crashing through the balsa wood and flattening a few dozen cardboard boxes. Heavy padding inside his costume helped to cushion him from the impact.

The director was not happy with the sequence. He suggested a few refinements. The giant stuntman did the fall three times before he got it absolutely right.

Valdano and Marie-Louise were relieved that the scene was over at last. It was a hot evening and they felt stifled in their costumes. They climbed down the rigging together. The Governor's daughter became Liza Davies again.

A mild argument developed.

'It can't do any harm, Max.'

'Yes, it could.'

'But Jenny's been asking me for days.'

'You could have said "no" to her.'

'That's not easy. Your daughter's very persistent.'

'I know,' agreed Max with a rueful smile. 'All I've said is that she can join me for a workout.'

'I'd prefer it if she wasn't encouraged, Liza.'

'But it's not encouragement. It might be just the opposite.'

'In what way?'

'You've seen my workout. It's very punishing. When Jenny realises how much slog is attached to the stunt business, she might think again.

Max Rawson considered the notion, then nodded.

'She might at that. Okay, let her join in.'

'I will.'

'And make her sweat, Liza. Show her what this business is like for a woman. Put her through all the hoops.'

'Leave it to me.'

They reached the deck and had a few words with the director about the scene they had just wrapped up. Technicians were milling around, putting their equipment to bed for the night. It was the end of a very long day and everyone seemed pleasantly exhausted.

Max and Liza soon joined the rest of the stunt team in the boat that would take them back to the *Florida Star* where they could change out of their costumes and remove their make-up. They sat together in the stern. Liza spoke first.

'Max.'

'Yes?'

'Suppose it doesn't work?'

'I don't follow.'

'What if the session with me only whets Jenny's appetite for coming into the business? I could guarantee that it would finish off most girls of her age, but she's rather special.'

'Very special,' confirmed Max with quiet pride. 'Jenny has a true sense of adventure. Can't resist a challenge.'

'I know someone else like that.'

He looked across at her and realised that she meant him.

They shared a laugh as the boat moved off.

The four of them sat around a table on the upper deck of the yacht. Nick, Jenny and Ed Garrett relaxed in chairs while Ernest chose his usual eccentric perch. Ernest was the old man's parrot. He was a large, alert bird with an orange beak and brightly-coloured plumage. Instead of resting on Ed's shoulder, he preferred to stand on his master's head. It was the reason that the old man always wore his cap.

'Abandon ship!' squawked the parrot. 'Women and children first!'

Ernest had a full repertoire of phrases and commands.

'Fire down below! Man the pumps!'

The parrot was named after Ernest Hemingway, the now legendary American writer who lived on Key West for a number of years and who wrote some of his novels and short stories there. Ed Garrett won the bird in a card-game that took place in Hemingway's favourite bar on the island. Hence the name Ernest. Man and parrot had now been together for decades.

'Clap on all canvas!' screeched Ernest.

'Quit bawling!' ordered his master. 'I'm trying to listen to what these kids are telling me.'

'That's about it, really,' said Nick, who had described the incident that afternoon. 'When I couldn't find anyone, we got into the boat and headed back here.'

'There never *was* a man with a white shirt,' affirmed Jenny.

'I saw him with my own eyes,' retorted her brother.

'Impossible! Isn't it, Ed?'

The old man scratched at his beard for a moment. He was not pleased to hear that they had ignored his advice and sailed due north and he had kept a grim face during their story. His features now split into the familiar gap-toothed grin.

'You did and you didn't see that man, Nick.'

'I'm not with you.'

'He wasn't really there.'

'Told you!' jeered the girl.

'But then again,' added the old man, 'he was.'

'I wish you'd explain,' said Nick.

'You saw a ghost out there.'

'A what?' Jenny was on the edge of her seat. 'A *ghost*?'

'How could it be?' countered her brother. 'No such thing.'

'That's where you're wrong, old buddy,' drawled Ed. 'There's a ghost on that island, okay, and you ain't the only person who's seen it. That guy's been waving his shirt for hundreds of years.'

Jenny was entranced. 'Who is he?'

'Ernest Hemingway!' answered the parrot.

'Scram!' yelled Ed.

He snatched his cap off to dislodge the bird, but Ernest was too quick for him. With a flap of his wings, he hopped on to the rail. After giving a loud squawk of disapproval, he began to preen himself.

Ed Garrett replaced his cap and scratched his beard again.

'All happened a long, long time ago, see?' he continued. 'In them days, a lot of pirates used to hang out in Key West. They'd pick off the ships coming into the Gulf and plunder them. That's why there are so many wrecks around here.'

'So who was the man with the shirt?' pressed Jenny.

'Name of Captain Arrighi. Italian pirate. God knows how he came to the Florida Keys but he did and he was a mean hombre. He was the guy who sank the *Seabird*.'

'The what?' said Nick.

'This French galleon. I don't speak the lingo so I can't tell you what it was really called. In English, it means Seabird. It went to the bottom over two hundred years ago and is lying out there near those islands you found.'

'And what happened to this Captain what's-his-name?' asked Jenny.

'I'm coming to that,' promised Ed, pausing to sip a glass of iced beer. 'His crew boarded the *Seabird*, stole everything she had, then sent her on her last voyage. Under the sea.'

Jenny's eyes widened. 'Was there much treasure?'

'Tons of it. That was the problem.'

'Problem?'

'Yeah,' explained Ed. 'Old Arrighi was one greedy son-of-a-gun. Wanted the biggest share for himself. Locked it all in his cabin and told his men he'd divide the spoils next day. Then he opened a cask of rum so that they could celebrate their prize. By nightfall, his crew were all good and drunk and tired. Arrighi waited until they were all fast asleep, then made his move.'

'What did he do?' said Jenny.

'Put all the really valuable stuff into a chest and took it ashore to one of the islands. Two guys helped him. He'd tipped them off before, so they made sure they didn't hit the rum too hard. The two men dig this hole and bury the treasure. Then their captain double-crosses them. Arrighi wanted to make sure that *he* was the only guy alive who knew where the stuff was hidden.'

Jenny was aghast. 'He *killed* them?'

'He shot one of them, but the other managed to get away. Took the boat and rowed back to the ship. He roused the crew and told them what had happened. They were pretty sore about it all.'

'I don't blame them,' remarked Nick. 'Did they go ashore and get the treasure back?'

'No,' replied Ed with a wry smile. 'They decided that if the captain wanted it that much, he could keep it. So they hoisted the sails and left him there all on his own. Arrighi never got off that island. Probably died of starvation. But his ghost still haunts the place. Trying to attract help. Lots of people reckon they've seen him waving this white shirt in the air. Today it was your turn, Nick.'

'That's marvellous!' said Jenny, believing every word.

Nick still had doubts. 'He didn't *look* like a ghost.'

'How d'you know if you never saw one before?' replied Ed.

'Was the treasure ever found?' wondered Jenny.

'No. It's still on that island somewhere.'

'How much is it worth now?'

'Millions of bucks, I guess.'

'Wow!'

'People have searched for it but it's closely guarded.'

'Who by?'

'Old Arrighi, of course.' Ed Garrett's voice became a sinister whisper. 'The Phantom Pirate.'

Ernest let out a shriek of fear that startled the children.

The Phantom Pirate.

Did he really exist?

Three

Buried Treasure

The short, tubby man in the crumpled white suit munched his food noisily, then washed it down with a mouthful of red wine. It was much cooler now, in the late evening, and he had stopped perspiring. During the heat of the day, it had never seemed to occur to him to slip off his coat or even to loosen his tie.

He reached for an apple and bit into it with relish.

'Delicious!' he announced.

Sitting on the ground opposite him was the older, grey-haired man whose hands were still tied behind his back although his gag had now been removed. He watched his captor with a blend of fear and resentment. The fat man scrunched his way through another piece of apple then gave an oily grin.

'Hungry, Mr Faulkner?' he mocked.

'What do you care?' rejoined the other.

'Oh, I care a lot. It is important you learn what it is like to go without food. When I was a boy - back home in Cuba - we had very little to eat.

While we were starving, rich Americans like you were living in luxury. It's not fair, is it?'

Faulkner said nothing. His captor had been goading him all day. The pangs of hunger were quite severe but he was not going to admit it. His throat was parched but he was determined not to beg for a drink. That would be a sign of weakness.

'What you did was a big mistake,' said the Cuban.

'I'll get out of this somehow,' vowed Faulkner.

'Yes. When *we* choose to let you go.'

'They'll find me sooner or later.'

'No, they won't,' insisted the other. 'You will not have another chance to wave your shirt like that.' He reached inside his coat and took out a small revolver. 'Next time you try anything, I use this. Understand?'

'I'm no good to you dead.'

'That will not stop me shooting you if I have to.'

Faulkner could see that his companion meant what he said. He was glad when the gun was put away in its holster. His only hope lay with two children who may or may not have seen his distress signal. It was very disheartening.

A distant sound revived his spirits and made him sit up. He could hear a motor launch approaching the island. The Cuban noted his reaction and sniggered.

'Sorry, Mr Faulkner. It's not the police come to save you. It is only Ricardo.' He threw aside the apple core. 'Wait till I tell him how naughty you were.'

The Cuban went out of the hideout and walked in the direction of the beach. A tall, muscular young man in slacks and a flowered shirt brought the launch into the shallows then switched off its engine. After throwing his anchor overboard, he jumped down into the water and waded ashore.

He saw his partner coming out of the trees and hurried towards him. Large gold-rimmed glasses hid eyes that were as cold as death. His tanned face was impassive. He did not seem to know how to smile.

Like his countryman, he spoke with a pronounced accent.

'Everything is going fine, Miguel.'

'Good.'

'I have given them some time to think it over.'

'Will they do as they're told, Ricardo?'

'Oh, yes,' said the other, grimly. 'I made sure of that.'

Miguel smirked. 'You have a way of putting these things.'

They turned and strolled back towards the hideout.

'Has Faulkner behaved himself?'

'Ah!' The fat man's smirk vanished at once. 'Trouble?'

'I turn my back for one minute. That is all.'

'What happened?'

Miguel recounted the incident with the shirt

and his companion's expression darkened. When they got to the hideout, Ricardo went in first and confronted the prone figure.

'You were warned, Mr Faulkner.'

'I've kept him tied up ever since,' explained his partner, following him in. 'He won't get away again.'

'I'll make certain of that,' promised Ricardo.

He bent down beside a black briefcase and opened it. Faulkner watched with growing apprehension as the tall Cuban brought out a syringe and a tiny bottle. When the syringe had been filled, the drug was injected into Faulkner's arm.

Within seconds it began to take effect. Faulkner became very drowsy and almost keeled over. Ricardo nodded to Miguel.

'Take off his ropes. We don't need them any more.'

Jenny Rawson lay in her bunk with her hands behind her head. All in all, it had been a good day. Her father had agreed to take her to Miami. Liza had said that she could join her in a workout, and there had been the fun of steering the boat for Nick.

What had really thrilled her, however, was Ed Garrett's story about the ghost. It was this which was keeping her awake well into the night. She was convinced that the old sailor's yarn was true. While their father was playing an imaginary phantom pirate in a feature film,

Jenny and her brother had stumbled on a real one.

It made the holiday seem more worthwhile than ever.

She was annoyed that she did not actually see the ghost herself, but that did not matter. The important part of the story was the bit about the buried treasure. Somewhere on the island was Captain Arrighi's chest, full to the top with untold wealth. All Jenny had to do was to find it. Her mind considered all the possibilities.

Before she finally dozed off, she set herself a target.

That buried treasure was going to be hers.

Nick Rawson was also unable to sleep but his thoughts took a different line. Though Ed Garrett's tale had sounded very convincing, the boy still had his reservations. The man on the island had not looked like a pirate. Although Nick had only caught a fleeting glimpse of him, he had seen the grey hair and the lean, tanned body.

Something else was worrying the boy but he did not know what it was. It remained niggling away at the back of his mind as he went over the afternoon's adventure once again. There *had* been someone on that island. Nick felt it. He had received a call for help and he wanted to answer it. Helping to rescue the man was his first priority and blocked out all thought of searching for any treasure.

He vowed that he would go back to the island somehow. Fatigue eventually began to catch up with him and his eyelids drooped. Then he was jerked awake again. At last he knew what had been troubling him. When he had seen the shirt being waved, he noticed something glinting on the man's wrist. He suddenly realised what it must have been and it proved conclusively that the figure was not a ghost.

No phantom pirate would have worn a wrist-watch.

There was definitely a human being on that island.

Nick would find him. Whatever the difficulties.

His hopes were dashed as soon as he came out on deck. Max Rawson saw at a glance that his daughter had not been put off by the severity of the morning workout with Liza Davies. Evidently Jenny was thriving on it. After going through some vigorous exercises and having a session with the weights, the girl was now trying to match the stuntwoman's skill on the trampoline.

Keeping to the middle of the canvas, Jenny bounced higher and higher until she had a regular, controlled lift. Then she did a somersault before landing on her feet again. Her success emboldened her to try a double somersault. This time she misjudged it slightly. Instead of hitting the trampoline with her feet, she ended up on her back. It made her giggle.

Liza was still panting from her own exertions. 'That was great, Jenny. Never thought you'd last the pace.'

'I'm nowhere near as fit as you,' replied the girl with renewed admiration for her friend. 'And I'll never be as good as you on the trampoline. Where did you learn all those tricks?'

'In the circus. You forget that I was brought up in a family of acrobats. I've been turning somersaults since I was about three.'

Max strolled across to them and smiled at his daughter.

'Well?'

'It was absolute torture, Daddy!'

'Serves you right.'

'Jenny did very well,' observed Liza. 'She's a natural gymnast.'

'Thanks,' said the girl, still gasping for air.

'You've only had one bash at it,' reminded her father. 'How would you fancy a workout like that every single day?'

'It would kill me!'

'Liza goes through that routine seven times a week.'

'Only way to keep strong and supple,' confirmed the woman.

'I never realised it would be so tough,' admitted Jenny.

'Does that mean you've changed your mind?' asked Max.

'Yes. I may not be a stuntwoman at all.'

'That's a relief.'

'I want to do what Liza did. Be a circus acrobat.'

Max gave a comic groan. Jenny and Liza laughed at him.

The stuntwoman then threw a towel around her shoulders.

'You'll have to excuse me while I take a shower,' she said. 'I have to be on set in an hour. The shark scene.'

'Captain Valdano versus Jaws,' noted Max. 'See you later.'

'And thanks a million!' added Jenny.

Liza smiled and strolled off to her cabin. Jenny took the chance to raise something with her father. She tried to sound as casual as she could.

'Didn't you tell me there was a lot of treasure around here?'

'Masses of it,' he replied. 'Thinking of diving for it?'

'No. I was just interested, that's all.'

'Ed Garrett is the man to talk to about treasure.'

'I know. We had a chat with him yesterday about the olden days. He said that dozens of ships were sunk in these waters.'

'That's right,' attested Max. 'Mostly Spanish galleons. Loaded up with gold and silver from their colonies in South America and the West Indies. The ships plied routes that skirted the southern coast of Florida so the pirates used to lie in wait and pounce.'

'It sounds terribly bloodthirsty.'

'It was, Jenny. Pirates were really dreadful characters who'd butcher passengers and crew to get their hands on the loot. There was no room for a Captain Valdano. True buccaneers were much more like Redbeard. Brutal, vicious and showing no pity for anyone.'

'What did they do with the treasure they stole?'

'Spent it, lost it, fought over it. Some of them buried it in secret places on the islands round here. If you knew where to dig, you could unearth yourself a fortune.'

'And would I be allowed to keep it if I did?'

'I don't see why not. Look at Mel Fisher.'

'Who?'

'The king of the treasure hunters,' explained her father. 'Ed knows him well. Fisher went diving after two famous Spanish vessels that went down in the seventeenth century. They were part of a fleet of warships that left Havana and got caught up in a hurricane. One was called the *Santa Margarita*, I think, but I can't remember the name of the other one.'

'Did this Mel Fisher find them?'

'In the end. Took him years and cost him a bomb, but his team of divers eventually located them. And what a haul they had!'

'What was it worth?' asked Jenny, eagerly.

'Millions and millions of dollars.'

'Gosh!'

'And there's even more still down there.'

'Is there?'

'According to Fisher. He estimated that there was a shipwreck for every quarter-mile of water along the Florida Keys alone. About ten per cent of them have treasure aboard.'

'How does he know?' pressed Jenny.

'Know what?'

'That some of those ships have gold and silver in them. I mean, how could he be sure there'd be so much treasure in those two Spanish galleons he found?'

Max shrugged. 'Easy. By checking the manifest.'

'The what?'

'It's a list of the ship's cargo. Fisher did his research very thoroughly and reaped the reward. Good luck to him.'

'What about the stuff buried on the islands?' probed Jenny.

'What about it?'

'If you knew what ship it came off, could you work out roughly how much there might be?'

'Of course. You'd need to search through the records. The library in Key West has got lots of material on it, if you want to know more. I've often thought of trying *my* hand at treasure-hunting. It's got the same kinds of risks as the stunt business, but you can make much more cash if you hit the jackpot.' He concentrated for a second then snapped his fingers. 'I know one book you might chase up. It's called *Lost*

Treasures of Florida's Gulf Coast. By a man called Hudson.'

Jenny was impressed. 'You know so much, Daddy.'

'Hardly surprising, is it?'

'No,' she said with a giggle. 'You're the Phantom Pirate!'

He swept her playfully up in his arms and dropped her gently on the trampoline. Jenny bounced away happily.

She had just been reminded of another aspect of the stunt world. The importance of research. Whenever her father was involved in a new project, he always took care to do some background reading beforehand. For the current film, he had clearly done his homework.

To Max Rawson, being a stuntman was not just a matter of attempting daring feats. It was an education.

He lifted his daughter off the trampoline.

'Enjoying the holiday now?'

'Best one we've ever had!' she decided.

Especially if she could track down that buried treasure.

The harsh drone of the outboard motor echoed in Nick's ear as his boat scudded along with its prow slicing through the water. A few seabirds trailed him but for once he ignored his feathered friends. His mind was fixed on one thing. Returning to the island.

He had been careful not to tell Ed that he

would be going back to the same place. The old sailor had been most insistent that he should keep away from that group of islands and instead explore those that were some miles due west of the *Florida Star*. Pretending to accept the advice, Nick had set off with the firm intention of forgetting it. He had altered course and now sailed north.

The voyage seemed to take a very long time and it was quite different without his sister. He felt lonely. At one point, when he could see no sign of land anywhere, he started to get strange fears. What would happen if he got lost, or if the engine gave out, or if the boat capsized? Nobody would have a clue where to look for him.

Nick began to question the wisdom of making the trip on his own. It might have been safer and more sensible to bring Jenny along but she had wanted to watch the filming of the shark scene.

Sharks!

His heart gave a jump as this new hazard suggested itself. His eyes roamed the sea anxiously in search of a tell-tale fin. He could not remember if there *were* any sharks in the Gulf of Mexico but he was taking no chances. He remained on the alert.

After what seemed like an age, a faint blur appeared in the far distance. He was on course for the islands. The sight of them restored his confidence. It also told him why he had chosen to make the journey alone.

Nobody else would take his version of the

story seriously. Ed had explained it away in terms of a ghost. The police would dismiss it as the fanciful invention of a lively young mind and even his father would be sceptical. Jenny had actually been there and refused to believe it.

It was a personal mission for Nick. The man had seen him and waved the shirt. Nick had a responsibility to the lone figure on the island. It was something which only he could discharge.

The motor continued to crackle away but land took a long while to approach. As the islands finally took shape before him, he tried to estimate how many there were in this particular group. Well over a dozen and scattered across an area of a few square miles. They all looked the same. Would he be able to find the right one again?

Frigate birds acted as his navigators once more. Two of them went soaring high above his head with effortless ease. As they began the decent towards their nests, they gave him his bearings. Nick recalled that one of the other islands was the home of a Great White Heron Refuge but he could not spare the time to investigate it now. Something else took priority.

Establishing contact with someone in distress.

He brought his boat in close, cut the motor then angled it up out of the water. After dragging the craft ashore, he went straight to the rocks again and climbed to the highest point. His binoculars examined the whole island without success.

Nick did not give up. He began a systematic search, zigzagging his way from one side to the other, poking between trees, looking under bushes and checking out every hollow or cavity in the ground. It was slow, methodical work but it bore no fruit.

Then he came to a small clearing and stood on a mound. He gazed out to sea and tried to imagine where his boat had been when he had first spotted the man. When he had done that, he used that location to give himself an idea of where the figure had been standing on the island.

In a clearing. On rising land.

He was probably at the exact point.

A surge of excitement gave him fresh encouragement and he started a detailed search of the ground nearby. This time his efforts were not in vain. Something else was now glinting in the sun.

A tiny silver button with a thread of white cotton.

He was certain that it was from the shirt.

Nick spent another hour carrying out an inspection of the immediate area. Though he felt that he was getting close to something, he never actually found it. At last he gave up and flopped down on the ground to rest from his hard work.

Several feet below him, lying in a drugged sleep, was the very man he sought. Miguel was standing beside him with his gun at the ready in case the hideaway was discovered. The intruder had got far too close for comfort. Sweat oozed freely from the fat Cuban.

Nick Rawson was blissfully unaware of the fact that he was sitting directly above a subterranean refuge. There was something else that he did not know.

Faulkner was a very exceptional man.

He was himself a kind of buried treasure.

Four

The Everglades

Marie-Louise tried to fight the men off but they were too strong for her. The pirates caught hold of her and flung her over the side of the ship. She hit the water with a resounding splash and she vanished beneath it. As soon as she came up again, she let out an ear-piercing scream.

A large fin was making its way towards her.

The Governor's daughter would be eaten by a shark.

She made desperate attempts to swim away but her heavy dress was an encumbrance. Death was imminent. She braced herself to feel the first savage bite.

Then Valdano swung into action. With a magnificent dive from the top of the mainmast, he plunged deep into the sea near the agonised Marie-Louise. Knife between his teeth, he surfaced just in time to do battle with the shark. It was a monster. He dodged its first thrust at him and managed to get an arm around it. Grabbing his knife with the other hand, he brought it down hard to inflict a wound in the under-belly.

The creature was enraged. It twisted and turned and arched its back in an effort to dislodge its attacker. But the Phantom Pirate was not easily shaken off. His knife struck again and again until the sea all around him turned red.

In a final, frenzied effort to get free, the creature dived for the ocean bed and took his passenger with him. Marie-Louise feared the worst. Valdano was under the water for far too long. She thought that he would never come up again.

Then something nudged her gently in the back.

'Oh!' she cried.

'Allow me to help you, Mademoiselle.'

'Valdano!'

She fainted dramatically into his arms.

The Phantom Pirate had won yet another marine encounter.

'That's it!' yelled the film director. 'Print it!'

The scene was over and ropes were thrown down to Max Rawson and Liza Davies and the couple were winched back up on to the deck of the sailing ship where warm towels, restorative drinks and a shower of congratulations awaited them.

A few minutes later, the shark was also winched aboard. It was a superb replica of the real thing, made out of rubber and powered by a small motor. It lay trembling on the deck with its jagged teeth bared in a fiendish grin.

What they had shot was only part of the sequence. The rest of it would be filmed in the swimming baths on Key West. Underwater heroics would be seen through the glass sides of the baths. The two scenes would then be cleverly spliced together in the cutting-room. The final result would convince the cinema audience that they had seen a genuine shark in a murderous battle.

Liza had enjoyed the dip. The sea was the ideal place to be on such a sweltering day. Wrapped up in her towel, she turned to Max.

'How many sharks does that make?'

'Heaven knows!' he replied. 'There was one part of my career when I seemed to kill about two in every film I did. I was typecast as the shark-fighter. I've also had a crack at an octopus, a sting ray, a giant eel and a whale.'

'Did you always win?'

'No. The whale swallowed me whole.'

'What we do to keep the audience entertained!'

'I know,' joked Max. 'But it beats working for a living.'

The Phantom Pirate was turning out to be fun.

Everybody seemed to be having a good time.

Even the shark.

Ed Garrett leaned over the rail and pointed across at the sailing ship. Ernest was perched on his cap and Jenny was standing beside the old sailor. Her knowledge was put to the test.

'Let's see if you remember what I taught you,' said Ed.
'All hands on deck!' shouted the parrot.
'Not *you*, Ernest!' roared his master.
'Land ahoy!'
Jenny giggled and then tried to be serious. Ed had told her the names of all the sails on the ship. When it was fully-rigged, there were twenty-eight. She did not know how she could possibly list them all. Jenny cleared her throat.
'Ready when you are, girl,' encouraged Ed.
'Where do I start?'
'At the front. With the flying jib.'
'Here goes then.' She used her fingers to count them off. 'The flying jib, outer jib, inner jib and jib. Foresail, lower fore topsail, upper fore topsail, lower fore topgallant sail, upper fore topgallant sail, fore royal.' She paused to inhale deeply. 'How am I doing?'
'Just keep going. And *faster*.'
She accelerated. 'Mainsail. Lower main topsail, upper main topsail, lower main topgallant sail, upper main topgallant sail, main royal, main skysail and...' Her tongue lost contact with the words. 'That's it!'
'You forgot the crossjack.'
'I know,' confessed Jenny. 'And the sails on the mizenmast.'
'Man overboard!' screeched Ernest.
'There'll be a parrot overboard if you don't quit that!' threatened Ed, flicking his cap. 'Now keep that beak shut. Hear me?'

‘We sail for Portobello in the morning!’

Jenny had now got used to the banter between Ed and his parrot. It kept everyone so amused that Ernest had now been given a part in the film, sitting on Redbeard’s shoulder in one scene. Ed was not altogether pleased about it and Jenny put this down to professional jealousy. The old man would dearly have loved to get in front of the cameras himself. He was a natural performer.

Nick came up on deck and crossed over to them.

‘How did the bird-watching go?’ asked Ed.

‘Fine.’ His tone was non-committal.

‘Did you sail due west like I told you?’

‘It was good advice,’ lied Nick. ‘I saw hundreds of birds.’

‘You should have seen the shark,’ Jenny told him.

‘I did. When they pumped it up.’

‘It looks so realistic in the water.’

‘I’ll stick with birds.’

‘Pity you haven’t gotten yourself up to the Everglades,’ remarked Ed, casually. ‘That’s the place for bird life.’

‘Yes,’ agreed the boy. ‘I’ve read about it. They say there are over three hundred species there.’

‘At least,’ confirmed the old man. ‘Not to mention some six hundred varieties of fish. It’s one helluva place, Nick. You’ll love it.’ A sly grin stole over his face. ‘Fancy a trip up there?’

Delight made Nick glow all over. He positively beamed.

'Do you really mean it, Ed?'

'Why not? Rest day tomorrow. Ideal time to go.'

'But it would take us hours by car.'

'Way I drive, son, it would take us *days*.'

'Batten down the hatches!' ordered Ernest.

'And I know one thing for sure!' bellowed Ed. '*You* ain't coming along with us to spoil the party.'

'Give us a kiss,' begged the parrot. 'Give us a kiss.'

'You're incorrigible, Ernest,' said Jenny.

Nick was still baffled. 'So how do we get there?'

'Same way as the birds.'

'We *fly*?'

'Chopper goes from Key West tomorrow morning. It'll drop us off at the Everglades and pick us up on the return run in the afternoon. How about it?'

'Count me in!' answered Nick with enthusiasm.

'What about you, Jenny?'

'No, thanks. Not my scene. Besides, I want to go to the library tomorrow and read up on a few things.'

'But you never open a book at home,' argued her brother.

'How do you know?' she challenged. 'You're

always too busy goggling through those flipping binoculars.'

'Seconds out – round one!' teased Ed.

'Fire a broadside!' squawked Ernest.

Ed held up an arm and the parrot hopped on to it.

'I'll see you guys later,' he said. 'Oh, and clear it with your father, won't you, Nick? About tomorrow.'

'Of course. Dad won't mind, I'm sure.'

'He'll be glad to get rid of him,' added Jenny.

Ed Garrett supplied his famous grin and walked away. Nick was overjoyed by the invitation. It even made him forget his trip.

'You went back, didn't you?' questioned his sister.

'What?'

'To that island.'

'Well...'

'It's okay. I won't tell Ed. You did, didn't you?'

'Yes,' he admitted.

'Did you see the ghost?'

'There *is* no ghost, Jenny,' he said with contempt. 'And there's nobody else there either. The island was deserted.'

'*I'll* be going back there soon,' she volunteered.

'Why?'

'You wait and see. But I'll tell you this, when I get there, I'll find what I'm after. Because I'll know where to look.'

Jenny spoke with complete conviction.

She had set her heart on finding the treasure.

Ricardo's eyes narrowed behind the gold-rimmed sunglasses. He almost spat out his questions at Miguel.

'When was this?'

'Earlier on.'

'He came alone?'

'Yes, Ricardo.'

'And you're sure it's the same boy?'

'Nick Rawson. That's what the girl called him the other time.'

'Then it's time we had a word with this Nick Rawson.'

'But he found nothing.'

'He came back, didn't he? That's enough for me.' He swung round to glare at his partner. 'Why didn't you do it when you had a chance?'

Miguel displayed his flabby palms in a gesture of helplessness.

'He was only a kid.'

'You're getting soft.'

'He knows nothing, I tell you. How can he?'

'So why does he have a second look?'

'Ricardo...'

The taller man dismissed his protest with a wave of his hand. He paced up and down on the little beach and considered the matter. At length he came to a decision.

'I will speak to Luis.'

'Do you *have* to?' said the other in alarm.

'Luis does what he's told. Unlike you.'

'That's not true. I follow your orders. What

have I done wrong?'

'Let that kid slip through your fingers.'

'He's nothing. Forget him.'

'I can't, Miguel,' snapped the other. 'You know what is at stake here. We have planned this for over a year. Nothing must get in our way. Nothing and nobody. Got that?'

'Yes, Ricardo,' muttered his companion, uneasily.

'I will not let some kid ruin everything. A couple of days is all we need, then we collect. If nothing trips us up.' He fingered his chin and lowered his voice. 'Luis will know what to do. We will have no more visits from this Nick Rawson.'

Miguel gulped. His perspiration flowed again.

The flight in the helicopter gave Nick an excellent opportunity to see the Florida Keys and their relation to each other. From the air he could identify the principal chain of islands, thirty-two in all, stretched out like washing on a clothes-line over a distance of a hundred miles. Linked by a series of spectacular bridges, the Keys formed a continuous line from Miami's Biscayne Bay to Key West itself.

Far over to Nick's left, among the pinheads that showed on the surface of the Gulf, was the island where he had witnessed the distress signal. He spared a thought for the man with the white shirt and speculated once more on who he could possibly be.

The noise of the helicopter made it necessary

for them all to wear special protection over their ears, so they were not able to chat on the way. As soon as they reached their destination, however, Ed and Nick made up for lost time.

'What about that, eh?' asked the old man.

'It was ace.'

'If I'd driven you in my truck, we'd still be down on Big Pine.'

'There's something I've been meaning to ask you, Ed. Why are they called Keys?'

'Comes from the Spanish word *cayo*,' explained the other. 'Means "little island". All those Keys in the chain yet they're as different from each other as cowboys from Indians. Each island has its own identity. There's Key Largo up this end and Key West down at the bottom but the two have very little in common.'

Nick let the old sailor ramble on. He was very grateful to Ed for bringing him to the Everglades and interested in everything that he had to say. The man was an inexhaustible source of information.

'How much d'you know about the Everglades?' asked Ed.

'Only what I've read.'

'All wrong, I daresay...'

Ed proceeded to give him a breezy lecture that combined hard fact with hilarious anecdote. Nick learned that the Everglades National Park at the southern tip of Florida covered an area of almost a million and a half acres. It was largely made up of an ocean of sawgrass that seems to go on for ever and which is only broken up by island hummocks of hardwood trees, sparse stands of cypress and slash pines and clumps of mangrove.

They could only hope to see a tiny portion of it and so they set out on one of the trails with a guide. There were several other people in the group, most of them with cameras or binoculars. One man had a video camera and kept asking the guide when they would find an alligator.

Ed and Nick meandered along at the back of the group. Neither of them paid any attention to the thickset young Cuban who was walking up ahead of them and who glanced back from time to time.

Nick was far too enchanted by the bird life to notice anything else. It was like strolling through a vast aviary. He constantly impressed Ed with his ability to pick out the different species.

'And what's *that* one?'

'A purple gallinule.'

'And that little fella?'

'Brown thrasher.'

'Ah!' said Ed. 'Even I know what *that* is.'

They had come upon a long, thin bird with striking plumage and a curious serpentine neck. Its jerky walk was very distinctive as it picked its way through the marsh. It was an anhinga.

'It's what I'd call a water turkey,' noted Ed.

'Otherwise known as a snakebird or an American darter,' added Nick. 'I've always wanted to see an anhinga. That one's a beauty.'

He recorded the details in his pad and did a brief sketch.

Ed and Nick were now dropping behind the others but they did not care. Neither did the young Cuban. He lurked in the undergrowth and kept them under close observation.

It was only a question of waiting for the right moment.

Jenny Rawson would never have believed that she could have enjoyed herself so much in a library. She tended to avoid books as much as she could at school and preferred to be in the gymnasium or out on the games field. But an hour in the library at Key West had given her a new respect for libraries. She was mesmerised.

They had everything she wanted. Jenny began with the book that her father had recommended and discovered a lot of advice for the novice treasure-hunter. There were examples of the markings that pirates used on trees to guide them to their treasure and there were plenty of other tips.

Armed with all this information, she felt much more confident about her ability to track down the booty that had once belonged to Captain Arrighi.

The search for details of the *Seabird* was equally fascinating. Spanish ships had dominated the Gulf in the sixteenth and seventeenth centuries and she learned that

L'Oiseau Marin, though built in France, had somehow come into Spanish hands. It sailed from the New World colony of Mexico in 1683 and was attacked by pirates north of Key West. *Seabird*, as Jenny thought of it, went down with all hands. The wreck was never found.

Her fingers were trembling with excitement as she turned the page and saw the ship's manifest. It listed wines, silks, velvet, taffeta and various other materials but she was not interested in that. Her eye went straight to its store of treasure.

Seabird had been carrying pearls, gold, silver, rubies, diamonds and a large quantity of plate. The estimated value at the time ran into thousands of pounds. Translated into modern currency, it would be worth millions.

'Wowee!' yelled Jenny to the surprise of all around her.

It was as if she had found the buried treasure already.

Nick Rawson, meanwhile, was engaged in research of his own. As they moved through swampy terrain, he noticed something that made him stop and kneel down. Ed walked on ahead and the boy was left alone.

It was like a scene out of a film. The coarse grasses seemed to be vibrating with a medley of sound. There were creaks and groans and strange whistles, the splash of jumping fish, the croaking of frogs and the droning of insects. The

Spanish moss that festooned the trees was like a giant cobweb across the marshes.

What Nick had spotted was the submerged, immobile body of an alligator, lying in wait for its prey. Birds, frogs and fishes came near to its great jaws but always turned away at the last moment. Then a family of anhingas appeared, moving in a flotilla towards the alligator and spearing small fish with their beaks. One of them dived underwater and came up with a juicy morsel of garfish.

As the adult birds paddled away from the alligator, one of the chicks remained to explore the marsh on its own. It went perilously close to the alligator whose patience was about to be rewarded. Nick was horrified at the thought that the innocent bird should be snapped up and he grabbed a twig to throw at the anhinga.

It splashed in the water and saved the bird's life.

Startled by the noise, the chick took fright and turned to hurry after its parents. The alligator had been deprived of an easy catch but a larger prey soon offered itself.

As Nick crouched down on the bank to watch the creature, he felt a hand in the small of his back. Before he could stop himself, he was pushed headfirst into the swamp. He went right under then fought his way back to his feet. The water only came up to his thighs.

Twenty yards away, the alligator was on the move.

It was stealthily closing in on him.
Nick was terrified.

Five

Danger Island

The alligator moved relentlessly forward with only its eyes and snout above the water. At first, Nick was completely petrified. His mind went blank, his limbs froze and his throat constricted.

Suddenly, he found his voice again.

'Help!!!!'

He had seen his father in the same situation many times and Max had always survived. But that was in films. The alligator was usually a model and the scene was always carefully rehearsed. If it did not work when the camera rolled, then it was easy to have another take.

Nick had to do without that luxury. He was up against the real thing and there was no time for rehearsal. If he did not get it right first time, there would not be a second.

'Ed! Quick!' he yelled. 'Help!'

He tried to wade to the bank but his feet got caught in the mud. The alligator was only yards from him now and the jaws would open any second. He looked around in a panic and saw a stout log floating nearby.

Making a dive for it, he scooped it up and used it to prod at the creature. The alligator surfaced properly and its mouth parted to expose rows of ugly teeth. Nick jabbed hard with the log and wedged it in between the jaws. With angry force, the animal closed its mouth and the wood cracked noisily.

But Nick had earned himself valuable seconds.

As the alligator tried to lose the obstruction by threshing its head about, Nick reached for an overhanging branch and swung himself up out of the water. When the pressure was really on, he could be almost as athletic as his sister. With his arms and legs curled around the branch, he worked his way along it until he was over solid ground again. Then he dropped back down.

He was still not out of danger, however. Furious at the loss of its prey, the alligator came surging out of the water with murderous intent and waddled up the muddy bank towards him.

Nick moved swiftly. He ran to the timbered walkway that had been built over this part of the swamp and scrambled up. Huge jaws snapped inches below his feet as he climbed, but he made good his escape. Shaken and exhausted, he sat down on the walkway to rest. The alligator could not reach him now. With a disconsolate flick of its tail, it scuttled off and vanished into the water again.

Voices were now heard and a few people from his group came running towards him. The guide got there first. He was a young man in shorts and T-shirt.

'We heard you yell for help. What happened?'

'I fell in by mistake.'

'Yeah. I can see that, buddy,' said the guide. 'You're supposed to stay on the walkway for safety along here. Don't you realise there are 'gators in that swamp?'

'I realise it now,' replied Nick with feeling.

They helped him up and expressed concern but he had suffered no real injury. There was one consolation. The pad in which he had jotted down all his notes was safe. He kept it in a waterproof cover whenever he went bird-watching near water. It had proved to be a wise precaution.

A new thought shot through his mind.

'Where's Ed?' he asked.

'Who?'

'I was walking along with him.'

'That old guy, you mean?'

'Yes. He couldn't have been far away when I stopped by that bank. He should have been first here when I called for help.'

The guide became alarmed. 'We'd better search for him.'

'Hey!'

Ed Garrett saved them the trouble. His voice came in a groan of pain.

'Over here!'

They rushed off in the direction of the cry. Nick forgot all about his own discomfort and led the race. They found Ed about thirty yards or so up the trail. He was lying full length in some bushes and had grazed himself badly as he fell. His hand was rubbing the back of his head.

Nick and the guide managed to sit him up.

'Are you okay, Ed?' asked the boy.

'Fine and dandy,' drawled the old man with a throaty chuckle... 'Just as well I got a thick skull, though. Must've slipped and banged it on something hard as I went down.'

'There's a big lump there,' noted Nick, examining the wound.

'If that's all the damage, I can live with it,' announced Ed with spirit. He looked at Nick properly for the first time. 'You been swimming or something?'

'I'll tell you later.'

'Too many accidents around here for my liking,' decided the guide. 'I'm supposed to be responsible for you guys' safety. From now on, we close up and stay together. Okay?'

Ed and Nick were happy to agree. They were soon fit to move on. The old man stuck to his story that he had inadvertently slipped but Nick sensed that he was concealing the truth. He suspected that the hand which had pushed him into the swamp had also dealt the blow which had felled Ed Garrett. The retired sailor had probably been knocked out first so that he would not be able to come to the aid of his friend.

Nick still shuddered when he thought about

his close encounter with the alligator but he made no mention of it to anyone else. He maintained that his fall had been quite accidental. Ed pretended to believe him and did his best to shrug the whole thing off.

'You got wet, I got a bump on the head. What's the harm?'

'None, really,' agreed Nick.

'We mustn't let it spoil our day out.'

But nevertheless it cast a shadow across the sun-blessed day. Nick's clothes soon dried out in the heat and the bird life continued to hypnotise him but it was not quite the same any more. Though he saw ibises, wood storks, limpkins, vermilion flycatchers, hooded warblers, the delightful roseate spoonbill and the rare Everglade kite, his mind always returned to something else he had seen.

An alligator. Face to face.

The significance of it all slowly dawned on him. Someone wanted him out of the way because he knew too much. The attack by the swamp was somehow linked with his two visits to an island to the north of Key West. Because one man had waved a white shirt at him, another had tried to kill him in the Everglades.

It made his blood run cold but it also reaffirmed an idea which had been steadily growing on him. He had to go back to that island. Instinct told him that the man was kept hidden on it somewhere. If the people holding him were prepared to go to such lengths to get rid of Nick, then the captive had to be highly important.

The boy had been scared but he had not been frightened off.

Like Jenny, he had inherited his father's iron determination. Rawsons were never deterred. They had a habit of seeing things through to the bitter end. It would take more than an unscheduled dip with a hungry alligator to stop him.

Nick would pay his third visit to the island next day.

Sitting on a bollard that overlooked the harbour, Jenny leafed through the pages of notes that she had made. It was not a bit like doing schoolwork. The hours in the library had flown past. It had been a labour of love and she now assessed the results.

She felt as if the *Seabird* were a personal friend now. Ideally, she would love to go scuba diving in search of the wreck itself. The vessel was lying in less than forty metres of water and she knew that it was in the vicinity of that group of islands.

But diving was a long and laborious business that took careful planning and special equipment. Jenny did not have the time or the means for it. She concentrated, therefore, on the thing she could do.

Find that buried treasure.

Like all fortune-hunters, she believed that it would be relatively easy once she got down to it. She would locate Arrighi's haul somehow. Then it was simply a question of digging. A few hours with a spade would make her impossibly rich.

The thought made her burst out laughing.

'What's so funny?' asked Liza, walking up to her.

'Nothing,' she replied, quickly covering up her notes.

'Been doing some homework, Jenny?'

'Not really.'

'What are you hiding there, then?' teased Liza. 'A love letter?'

'Of course not!' snorted the girl with disgust.

'Don't you like boys?'

'Not in that way. It's soppy.'

'Times have changed,' sighed Liza. 'When I was your age, all I could think about was getting my first boyfriend. And my first passionate love letter.'

Jenny's annoyance lessened and she glanced around to make sure that nobody could overhear them. Then she confided something to her friend.

'I did get a Valentine card this year.'

'Lovely! Who sent it?'

'I don't know. It wasn't signed.'

'Didn't he give you a clue?'

'No. I waited and waited but nothing happened.' It was her turn to sigh. 'The truth is, I think I frighten boys off.'

'It's because you can do everything better than they can.'

'That's true!' agreed Jenny, giggling.

She folded up the papers in her hand and slipped them into her pocket. Then she became thoughtful. She decided it was the moment to raise something rather private.

'Liza...'

'Yes?'

'How long have you known Daddy?'

'Four or five years, I suppose. Ever since we worked on that film about Ivanhoe. He rescued me about ten times in that.'

'And you've always got on very well with him, haven't you?'

'Max Rawson is the best in the business,' asserted Liza. 'It's always a pleasure to work with him.'

'I wasn't talking about work.'

'Oh. I see.'

Liza knew what was coming. She had to suppress a smile.

'Daddy is ever so fond of you,' continued Jenny. 'He thinks you're smashing. So do we – and that's vital.'

'I'm glad I get the Rawson seal of approval.'

'It goes deeper than that with Daddy. In fact...' She hesitated for a few moments then blurted it out. 'Have you ever thought of marrying him?'

'Naturally.'

Jenny was thrilled. 'You *have*?'

'Yes,' admitted Liza, cheerfully. 'So have dozens of other women, I daresay. Max Rawson is a very eligible man. Handsome, successful, sound in wind and limb. Oh, yes - and he has these two great kids.'

'Marry him,' urged the girl. 'Why don't you?'

'Lots of reasons. The main one is that he hasn't asked me.'

'Oh, he will,' insisted Jenny. 'Leave that to us. We'll *make* him.'

'That's very kind of you,' said Liza with a broad grin, 'but I don't want a husband who's been dragooned into marriage. To tell you the truth, I don't want a husband at all. Not yet, anyhow. I like my independence too much. Your father and I are... just good friends.'

'Pity. It would have made such a difference.'

Liza nodded sadly. She knew that Max's wife had died tragically not long after the children had been born. He had brought them up on his own and it had been something of a struggle, given the nature of his work. But he had made an excellent job of it.

Inevitably, however, they missed having a mother. She could understand Jenny's willingness to audition prospective candidates for that role and she felt honoured that she was one of them.

The girl read her thoughts and then surprised her.

'It's not because of *us*, Liza.'

'Isn't it?'

'Oh, no,' explained the girl, airily. 'We can manage very well on our own. Like you, we want our independence. It's Daddy I was thinking about. He needs a wife.'

'Does he?'

'Well, put it this way. It would be a big help to us if he had one. Then he wouldn't worry about us so much. At the moment, he tries to be father and mother to us and it's not possible. If he married again, he'd have someone who'd stop him from getting under our feet.'

Liza could contain her mirth no longer.

Jenny Rawson was nothing if not frank.

Ed Garrett sent word that he would not be able to sail out with the *Florida Star* next morning. He had suffered a reaction to the bump on his head and was staying in bed. Nick was puzzled by the news. He did not think there was anything that would have kept Ed away from a day's filming.

As he got the boat ready, he asked himself another question. A deliberate attack was made on him in the Everglades. How did his assailant know that he would be there? Indeed, how did the man know who he was in the first place?

Nick recalled the first visit to the island. Jenny had called out his name so his identity had been disclosed to anyone listening. Again, the boat bore the same name as the yacht so it was evident that he was involved with the film company in some way.

But that did not account for the presence of an

attacker at the Everglades. Someone must have tipped him off. Apart from his family and Liza, only one person knew that he would be flying off for the day in the helicopter.

Ed Garrett himself.

Nick was jolted. He refused to accept that his friend had betrayed him and yet there were definite grounds for suspicion. Why had Ed drifted away from him in the Everglades? By leaving the boy on his own near the swamp, he exposed him to the attack.

And what of the old man's own injuries? Had he really been struck down from behind by an unseen hand? Was there, in fact, a third person at all? Nick found himself wondering if it had been Ed himself who had shoved him in with the alligator. Could his friend's wounds have been self-inflicted?

Then there was the island.

Ed had done his best to stop them from sailing north to that particular group of Keys. When Nick had come back with his tale of a man in distress, the old sailor had explained it away as a meeting with a ghost. The boy hated to admit it but Ed Garrett was a prime suspect. At the very least, he had wilfully misled them.

Why?

The answer – like so many others – lay out on the island.

'Sorry to keep you waiting, Nick.'

'Where on earth did you get *that*!' he exclaimed.

'I borrowed it from the props people,' said Jenny, lowering the rustic spade into the boat. 'It's the one they use for the burial scene in the film.'

She had brought other equipment as well. An axe, a rope, a ball of string and some small tent pegs. The fruits of her research at the library were tucked away in her pocket.

Jenny also brought unbounded enthusiasm.

'Get me there as soon as you can. I want to *dig*!'

'We're going to the island to find that man,' insisted Nick.

'Not me. I'm after his treasure.'

'I keep telling you. That was no ghost.'

'That's a matter of opinion.'

'He was wearing a *watch*, Jenny.'

'Even ghosts need to know what time it is.'

Nick gave up. Nothing would stop Jenny's treasure hunt. He was simply grateful for her company. If there was trouble when they got there, she would not let him down. He drew comfort from this.

They set sail and headed due north. Jenny pondered.

'Do you think we should have told Daddy the truth?'

'No. He'd have stopped us going.'

'He wouldn't have stopped me digging for pirate gold. Daddy would have let me go ahead then laughed at me when I came home with nothing but blisters on my hands.'

'He'll still do that,' warned Nick.

'I'll show him,' she vowed. 'And you.'

'Don't bank on that.'

As they moved on, she wrestled with a moral dilemma.

'I don't like telling him lies.'

'We didn't tell him lies,' corrected Nick. 'We just sort of held back the truth.'

'What's the difference?'

'Look, it's vital that I get to that island. I didn't want to get bogged down in long explanations to Dad. He'd have called in the police and we'd have missed out on all the fun.'

'Not to mention all the treasure!'

Nick smiled. His sister was counting the haul already.

The islands seemed further away than ever this time and Nick's impatience grew. He was soothed by the sight of a frigate bird. Jenny let him steer and spent the voyage consulting her notes.

They reached the island at long last and Nick took the boat in to the same landing place. When they had beached the craft and unloaded the equipment, they walked towards a clump of trees.

Jenny dropped her spade and ran to embrace a gnarled trunk.

'Here it is!' she decided. 'My first clue.'

'What are you on about?'

'These tree markings. See?' She pointed to a pattern that was gouged in the trunk. 'That's a pirate sign.'

'Rubbish.'

'It might even have been carved by Captain Arrighi.'

'Jenny,' he argued, 'if he really did come on this island, it was over three hundred years ago. These trees haven't been here that long. So how did he manage to put those markings there?'

Her face fell but her optimism shone through at once.

'Maybe his ghost did it.'

She ignored his mocking grin and set to work. She used the tent pegs to mark out the area for digging then joined them with the string. After spitting on her hands, she took hold of the spade and jabbed it down with real purpose. The ground was hard and dry and unyielding. It was not going to be easy.

Nick left his sister at it and went off on his own search. He began at the place where he had found the shirt button and he had a long pole to help him this time. It enabled him to probe into hidden corners and lift thick undergrowth.

Oblivious to the perils that awaited them, they worked on. Neither of them met with any real success but that only made them try harder. Each had come to the island with a specific goal in mind. They did not want to leave until they had attained those goals.

Jenny dug on and Nick thrust away with his pole.

Both felt they were on the brink of discovery.

Ricardo put the coins into the public telephone and dialled the number that he now knew by heart. The receiver was picked up immediately at the other end of the line and the hoarse voice of a distraught, middle-aged woman was heard.

'Is that you?'

'It's me,' he confirmed.

'How is he? Can I speak to him?'

'No - but he's fine.'

'When can I see him?' she begged.

'When you make the drop. Have you got everything?'

'Yes.'

'Are you sure?' he pressed.

'Everything you asked for. It's all here.'

'And you've told nobody?'

'Of course not. I wouldn't dare.'

'If I find out the cops are in on this...'

'They're not,' she promised with obvious sincerity. 'I did exactly as you told me. *Exactly*. All I want is to have him back.'

'You will, Mrs Faulkner. Tonight.'

'Where? What time?'

'I'll be in touch.'

Ricardo hung up the receiver and went back into the bar. He had another drink and chatted amiably with a young, thickset Cuban. An hour later, they walked into a bar on the other side of Key West. Ricardo went straight to the public telephone and inserted some coins. He rang the same number. Response was instant.

Her voice was now close to hysteria.

'Is that you again?'

'Listen carefully.'

'I will, I will.'

'These are your directions. I only give them once.'

'I'm ready,' she gasped.

'Get it right and we trade,' said Ricardo, coolly. 'Foul it up and you'll never see him alive again.'

There was a sharp intake of breath at her end of the line.

'Okay, Mrs Faulkner. Let's get on with it.'

'Yes...'

'Here are your directions...'

He spoke slowly and emphatically then put the receiver down. By that night it would all be over. Ricardo had brought it off. It deserved a celebration. He crossed to the bar and bought another round of drinks. The men toasted their success. Ricardo relaxed.

'You haven't told me how you bumped off the kid, Luis.'

'Alligator. He had no chance.'

'That's the last we'll be hearing of him, then.'

'Oh, yes. He's gone for good.'

Heat and disillusion finally caught up with her.

A strenuous hour or more with the spade had given Jenny a pain in her back and a burning sensation in her palms. All she had to show for her endeavours was a series of shallow holes in the ground. No treasure.

She began to have second thoughts about it all.

Nick, by contrast, was quite encouraged. Vigorous use of the pole had uncovered all kinds of nooks and crannies. The island was full of potential hiding places.

He reached the area where he had flopped down to rest on his previous visit. The vegetation surrounding it was matted and he had to wield the pole with full force. As he thrust it into one bush, he found a large cavity concealed behind it. He knelt down to investigate and saw that a small ladder had been fixed to the side of the cavity and that it gave access to an underground cabin.

Nick stood up to call Jenny and turned round.

A revolver was staring him in the face. It was held by a short, tubby man in a crumpled white suit.

Miguel's dark moustache twitched by way of welcome.

'Hello,' he said. 'Want to see inside?'

Six

Hostages

Faulkner lay on his mattress in a drowsy half-sleep. He had been given enough water to sustain him but very little food. He was pale and drawn. When he heard feet descending the ladder outside, it was the most he could do to flick open his eyes.

Nick was pushed into the cabin by a fleshy hand. He recognised Faulkner at once as the man who had waved the shirt and he crossed to bend over him.

'Get away!' ordered Miguel.

'What's wrong with him?'

'Nothing - now stand back!'

He used the gun to motion Nick against one wall. The boy took the opportunity to glance around. He was inside a cabin that was made out of some light alloy. It fitted perfectly into the cavity below the ground and its entrance had been cunningly disguised above.

The cabin was small but quite self-contained. It had two mattresses, a table and two chairs, some boxes of tinned food and a few bottles of wine. Cigarette stubs littered the floor and Nick noticed something else lying amongst them.

Plastic, throw-away syringes. The prisoner was drugged.

Miguel kicked some ropes towards the boy.

'Tie your feet together.'

'Why?'

'Do as I tell you,' he snapped. 'Would you rather *I* did it?'

He raised the butt of his gun in a threatening gesture. Nick understood. He had no wish to be knocked out and then tied. He sat down and got to work with the rope. Miguel supervised him.

'Tighter,' he insisted.

'It is tight.'

'Hands behind your back. Quick!'

Nick obeyed and the Cuban bound his wrists with speed. He came to stand in front of the boy and looked down at him in triumph.

'Now for the girl.'

'You leave Jenny alone!'

'I won't be long.'

Miguel went out of the cabin and climbed the ladder. Nick struggled to break free from the ropes but it was hopeless. He was trussed up too securely.

Faulkner came awake for a second and whispered his need.

'Water...'

Nick swallowed hard and watched the man with compassion.

*

Miguel moved as silently through the undergrowth as his bulk would allow. He knew the general area in which Jenny had been working and he skirted it so that he could come up behind her and have the advantage of surprise. He did not foresee any trouble. After all, she was only a girl. He would not even need to use his gun.

Creeping low through the trees, he made the cover of some bushes and inched his way along behind them. Jenny was now quite close. She had started digging again and he could hear the grating noise of the spade. When he got to the end of the bushes, he stood up, expecting her to have her back to him. Instead of that, she was at the ready.

As soon as his head lifted above the bushes, she swung her implement. It caught him a glancing blow on the temple and knocked him senseless. Jenny was on him like a flash. She took his gun and held it nervously on the palm of her hand as if expecting it to go off. Then she raced to the spot where she had last seen her brother.

She tramped around in the undergrowth.

'Nick!' she called. 'Can you hear me?'

'Down here!' came a distant yell.

'Where?'

'Search the bushes! There's a way down!'

The muffled sound seemed to come from directly beneath her. Jenny did as she was advised and she soon stumbled on the secret entrance. She whistled in admiration at its cleverness.

'What are you doing?' shouted Nick.

'I'm coming, I'm coming.'

She went quickly down the ladder and into the cabin. The first thing that hit her was the sight of Faulkner stretched out on the mattress. She could see that he was very weak.

'Who is he?'

'I don't know. I think they've kidnapped him.'

'That fat man tried to kidnap me,' she said, defiantly. 'I clonked him with the spade. That'll teach him.'

'Untie me, Jenny.'

'Oh, sorry.'

She hurriedly undid the ropes that held his wrists and he set to work on his other bonds himself. Faulkner, meanwhile, was mumbling about water again. Jenny found a mug and poured water into it from a bottle. She lifted Faulkner's head up so that he could sip the liquid. He murmured his thanks.

Nick was now free again. He got up and collected the ropes.

'We'll have to tie *him* up now. Where did you leave him?'

'I'll show you.'

'Lead the way.'

'Wait a minute. You'd better have this.' She passed the revolver to him. 'I've no idea how to use this.'

'Neither have I,' he confessed.

'The fat man doesn't know that, though, does he?'

'Good thinking.'

He thrust the gun into his belt and followed her up the ladder. Nick was grateful that Jenny had come with him on this third visit. On his own, he had been overpowered with ease. It was his younger sister who had rescued him. With a spade in her hands, she had been a match for a ruthless criminal.

It made him feel proud of her.

They reached ground level again.

'This way,' she said, breaking into a run. 'Not far.'

'I'm right behind you.'

Jenny sprinted down past the bushes and out into the clearing where she had been digging. But Miguel was nowhere to be seen. He had clearly not been unconscious for very long.

A high-pitched noise explained where the Cuban was. He was starting up the outboard motor on their boat. Jenny was livid.

'He's pinching it!'

'Let's stop him.'

They charged off down the beach at full pelt.

'Come back!'

'That boat belongs to us!'

'Stop!'

'I'll shoot if you don't!'

But the boat was already carving a way for itself through the foam-capped waves with the sweating Miguel aboard. His journey was a short one. As soon as he was a few hundred metres from shore, he cut the engine and let the boat drift.

'What's he doing?' asked Jenny.

'Waiting.'

'What for?'

'Help, probably,' said Nick. 'The main thing is that we're stuck here now. We're trapped.'

It was a chilling thought.

A long day had begun very early for Max Rawson and his stunt team. They had been hard at it for several hours when the lunch break finally arrived. The meal was eaten on the upper deck of the *Florida Star* and the seafood won many compliments.

Max shared his usual table with Liza Davies.

'When did the children say they'd be back?' he wondered.

'They didn't.'

'I hope it's not too late.'

'Don't worry about them. They can take care of themselves.'

'You sound like Jenny.'

'She did coach me a bit, I must admit.'

'Did she suggest that you should marry me?'

Liza smiled. 'Yes, she did as a matter of fact.'

'I wish she'd stop doing that. It gets embarrassing.'

'How many wives has she lined up for you so far?'

'About twenty. Anyone would think I was a Sultan.'

They carried on with their meal and talked about the scene they had been filming that morning but Max was not able to dismiss the children from his mind. He soon worked them back into the conversation.

'Where have they gone exactly?'

'Bird-watching.'

'But where?'

'Same place they went before, I suppose,' guessed Liza. 'All I know is that they were as keen as anything to get going. Especially Jenny.'

'Since when has she taken up bird-watching?'

'Ask her when she comes back.'

'I will.' Max had a long drink of iced orange juice. 'I'd feel a lot happier if someone had gone with them. Ed Garrett, for instance.'

'He's off colour.'

'So I hear. What's the trouble?'

'Delayed shock from that bump he had in the Everglades.'

'Yes,' grumbled Max. 'I'm not convinced that I heard the full truth about *that* little escapade either.'

'Your children are young adults,' she urged. 'Give them some freedom. Compared to many kids today, they're very responsible.'

'I know,' he conceded, 'and I do fuss over them like a mother hen sometimes. It's ridiculous but I just can't help it.' He tried to reassure himself.

'Still, they can't do much damage on a bird-watching expedition. That's something.'

'They're having a whale of a time if I know them,' added Liza. 'I only wish I was with them. Nick and Jenny are having all the fun.'

Faulkner was now sitting up on the mattress with his back against the wall of the cabin. A fresh drink of water and a few slices of apple helped to rally him slightly but the drug had left him both confused and debilitated. The children tried to coax information out of him but it was proving difficult.

'What is your name?' asked Jenny.

'Faulk . . . ner.'

'Can you remember what happened, Mr Faulkner?'

'Kid . . . nap.'

'When?'

He shook his head very gently to indicate that he did not know. The drug had destroyed his grasp on time. Day and night had blended into one and he had lost all his bearings.

Nick took a hand in the questioning, speaking in a whisper.

'Why did they kidnap you, Mr Faulkner?'

'Ran . . . som.'

'What sort of ransom?'

The man opened his mouth to speak but the words would not come. He summoned up all his energy and tried again but only one thing came from his trembling lips.'

'Sea . . . bird.'

'Seabird?' repeated Nick.

'Does he mean that French ship?' wondered Jenny.

Faulkner could only mouth the word this time.

'Sea . . . bird.'

His eyes rolled and his head lolled. He was alseep again. Nick helped him to lie down on the mattress then soaked his handkerchief in cold water and made a compress to put on the man's forehead. He had read the signal of the waving shirt rightly.

Faulkner was in distress. His condition was serious.

The children gazed down at him in sympathy.

'Still believe in ghosts now?' challenged Nick.

'No,' admitted Jenny. 'Nor in buried treasure.'

Ed Garrett sat in his little cottage on Key West and stared deep into his glass of rum. Perched on the back of a chair, Ernest talked to himself in a private language. The afternoon sun was beginning to slant in through the windows. Sounds of traffic and bustle could be heard in the narrow street outside.

The bump on his head was still throbbing but it was not the reason that Ed had taken a day off work. He wanted time to brood on something. A case of divided loyalties.

Max Rawson had been very kind to the old sailor in the time they had worked together and the stuntman's children had been a joy to befriend. Until they made the mistake of sailing due north on that first fatal outing.

Guilt nibbled away at Ed as he recalled the incidents in the Everglades. He was convinced that Nick had been in serious danger and it had all been his fault. Indirectly.

He brooded on, then came to a decision. Throwing the last of the rum down his throat, he crossed to a sideboard and opened the drawer. An old cigar box was held together by an elastic band. He slipped off the band and lifted the lid.

Crisp twenty dollar notes were revealed. He counted them.

Miguel did not know whether to be glad or frightened when he saw the motor-launch coming. Ricardo was not going to be pleased to hear that his partner had come off worst against two young teenagers. On the other hand, Miguel had managed to keep them virtual prisoners on the island. More important, Faulkner was still there.

When the launch got close, Ricardo switched the engine to idling speed and drifted alongside the boat. His fury was unmistakable.

'What the hell is going on, Miguel!'

'Those kids,' gulped the other. 'They came back.'

'*Both* of them?'

'Yes.'

'But Luis swore to me that he'd finished the boy off! Why can't any of you do a job properly. I work with numskulls!'

'Sorry, Ricardo.'

'So why are you *here* when they are on the island?'

'You are not going to like this...'

Miguel guessed right. His senior partner hated all that he was told. Careful planning had been ruined. A foolproof scheme was now in jeopardy. Ricardo fought hard to stop himself from attacking his fat colleague.

In the end, he calmed down and considered his next move.

'We go to the island,' he announced.

'But they have my gun, Ricardo.'

'Then we take it from them. They are only kids.'

'That's what I think till that girl hits me.'

'*I'll* hit you if you let me down just once more.'

'Yes, Ricardo.'

The boat was tied to the rear of the motor launch and towed in towards the island. Ricardo anchored a short distance from the shore then explained his plan to Miguel. They jumped into the water and paddled to the beach.

The two men split up and made their way cautiously towards the trees. Even in the subterranean hideaway, the children must have heard the approach of the motor launch. They would be on the alert. Therefore extra care was needed. Nick was armed and Miguel could vouch for the fact that Jenny knew how to swing a spade. The fat Cuban's head was still ringing.

They reached cover, exchanged a signal, then crept furtively on. Ricardo was holding a Smith and Wesson automatic pistol and Miguel had a long knife at the ready. They had fanned out so that they could converge on the hideaway together.

Their fears of an ambush were groundless. The children did not try to take them by surprise and this gave the men increased confidence. Slowly and remorselessly, they moved in.

When they got to the entrance to the hideaway, Ricardo sat on the edge of the cavity and tensed himself for action. With cat-like agility, he leapt into the hole and landed at the bottom on his feet.

Gun held before him, he charged into the cabin.

'Hands up or I'll shoot!'

'Well done!' congratulated his partner from above.

But Ricardo was dismayed. Instead of capturing two teenage children, he was pointing his weapon at an empty cabin. Miguel came pounding down the ladder.

His astonishment was just as great.

'Where have they gone?'

'Not very far,' noted Ricardo. 'Faulkner is heavy. Come on.'

He raced up the ladder with Miguel close behind him.

Nick, Jenny and Faulkner were less than fifty

metres away. They were lying side by side in a shallow depression that was covered by a mass of thick vegetation. Nick had discovered it earlier when he was exploring the island. It had been impossible to drag their cargo any further away in the time. Faulkner was indeed heavy. They had exhausted themselves simply getting him out of the cabin. Taking him to a new hiding place had taxed them both and they were breathing heavily and were covered in perspiration.

'I feel like a sardine,' whispered Jenny.

'Shhhh!'

Nick could hear the two men talking to each other as they conducted their search. Their only hope was to lie motionless and be absolutely silent. Faulkner murmured beside them then lapsed back into his half-sleep.

Footsteps came nearer and nearer and their nerves went as taut as bowstrings. Through a tiny gap in the leaves, Nick could actually see Ricardo's feet. They were almost within reach.

After probing all around, the kidnappers decided to widen the area of their search and started to move away. Nick and Jenny were suffused with relief but, unfortunately, it did not last.

'Sea . . . bird.'

Faulkner's voice was faint but it was nevertheless picked up. With brutal thoroughness, Ricardo grabbed hold of the main bush that hid them and tugged it back. The three of them were revealed.

Nick tried to aim the gun but Ricardo kicked it from his hand with a swift flick of his foot. Miguel reclaimed his weapon with glee then pointed it down at the three cowering figures.

'So,' said Ricardo. 'You like to play hide and seek.'

'We know what *you* like to play,' retorted Jenny. 'Kidnapping.'

'Get Faulkner out of there,' ordered the tall Cuban.

Miguel obeyed at once, holding the limp figure under the armpits and pulling him out unceremoniously on to open ground. The children were made to get up and stand in front of a tree. They were still looking down the barrel of the automatic pistol.

Ricardo was a stern interrogator.

'Who else knows that you came here?'

'Nobody,' replied Nick.

'Don't lie to me!' snarled the other.

'It's not a lie.'

'You told your father,' accused Ricardo.

'I didn't.'

'Tell the truth!'

'He'd never have allowed us to come here.'

'What did you say to him?'

'Everything!' rejoined Jenny with bravado, trying a new tack. 'He knows where we are and what your game is so you might as well give up now. Daddy will be here any minute with the police and you won't have a chance. So there!'

Miguel burst out laughing and even Ricardo smiled.

'Now we *know* the boy was not lying,' observed the latter. 'You came on your own. Without telling anyone. That is good. For us, anyway. But not for you.'

'What are we going to do with them?' asked Miguel.

'Pity there are no alligators on the island,' said his colleague.

'Alligators!' Jenny went white.

Nick remembered the Everglades. He now knew who had set up the attempt on his life. Ricardo nodded in agreement.

'Yes, my young friend. *I* gave the command.'

'Thanks to Ed Garrett,' commented Miguel.

Jenny was shocked to hear the name. She had trusted the old man implicitly and grown fond both of him and of his parrot. She was horrified to learn that Ed was involved with the kidnappers.

Nick's sense of betrayal was even sharper. Ed had effectively set him up for attack by taking him to the Everglades. The boy's reluctant suspicions were all justified.

'So what do we do with them?' pursued Miguel.

'We keep them,' decided his colleague.

'Keep them?'

'As hostages. In case we hit trouble.'

'Shall I tie them up, Ricardo?'

'No need.'

'Why?'

'I have a better idea. We do not have to hold on to Faulkner much longer. If all goes well, the drop takes place tonight. We hand him back to his wife. What's left of him.'

Faulkner stirred at the mention of his wife and tried to say something but they could not make out the words. Miguel was still slightly puzzled.

'What is this better idea of yours, Ricardo?'

'Until tonight, we move to another island. You, me, Faulkner.'

'And the kids?'

'I know the perfect place for them.'

Max Rawson made a point of getting to know the names of everybody working on the film and he always had a cheery greeting for them if their paths crossed. Fiona was a short, vivacious girl with long brown hair and a patchwork of freckles on her pleasant face. She had responsibility for the many hundreds of props that were used in the film. She was always rushing around with an armful of swords or tankards or sheets of parchment.

Max bumped into her on the poop deck of the sailing ship.

'Hello, Fiona.'

'You were fantastic in that last scene, Max.'

'Thanks. Couldn't have done it without you and your props.'

She smiled. 'How did Jenny get on?'

'Get on?'

'That treasure hunt of hers,' explained Fiona. 'At least, I assumed that's what it was. Why else would she want to borrow a spade from me?'

'First I've heard of any spade.'

'She begged me to loan it to her. In the end, I said I would.'

Alarm bells rang.

Max recalled her sudden interest in buried treasure and her willingness to spend a blazing hot day in the Key West library. She would certainly not need a spade to go bird-watching.

'Why didn't she tell me she was going on a dig?' he wondered.

'You know Jenny,' she replied. 'A law unto herself sometimes.'

Anxieties multiplied inside his head.

Where exactly *were* his two children?

Jenny held the mattress upright against the door and Nick hurled himself at it yet again. It was all in vain. The door held. He was too much out of breath to try any more.

His sister took over and the thick mattress took the sting out of the impact but she made no headway. Their prison was secure. The Cubans had locked them inside the cabin. Though it was only constructed out of an alloy, it was surprisingly tough. Five of its sides were hard up against solid earth and there was no hope of forcing a way out.

That left the door. It seemed impregnable.

After locking it from outside, the men had wedged a heavy log under the door handle. It was an additional buttress that held firm. Half an hour of attack had made no impression on the door.

Jenny threw the mattress to the floor and dropped down on it.

'I wish I'd hit the fat one much harder with that spade.'

'There *has* to be a way out somehow,' mused Nick.

'We're trapped in here till they open that door,' she complained then she sat up with a start. 'Suppose they don't?'

'Don't what?'

'Come back. They said they would but they could have been bluffing. Do you realise what would happen, Nick? We'd *never* get out of here!'

'Of course we would,' he reassured. 'Someone will find us.'

'How?' she wailed. 'Not a soul knows we're down here.'

Nick shuddered as he saw the implications.

They could be buried alive.

Seven

Taking Risks

Miguel used his binoculars to study the horizon. He shook his head.

'Nothing.'

'We had to be sure.'

'Why did we come across to this island?'

'Precaution. If someone *does* come looking for those kids, we don't want to be in the same place as they are.'

'You think of everything, Ricardo.'

'Somebody has to do the thinking round here.'

They left the small promontory and walked back to where Faulkner was sitting. Now that the effect of the drugs was wearing off, he was feeling much better though he remained weak. His back was resting against a tree.

'How you feel now, Mr Faulkner?' asked Ricardo. 'Ready to go back home to your little wife?'

'Shut your mouth about her,' warned the American.

'But she is the only person who can save you.'

'Ricardo has been chatting to her on the phone,' said Miguel.

'Yes,' added his partner. 'She understands the position.'

Faulkner bit back a reply. There was no point in antagonising them any further. At the moment, they held all the cards.

'Think she'll do as she's told?' asked Miguel.

'Oh, yes. I put the fear of death into her.'

'How can we be certain, though?'

'Luis will take care of that. As soon as she leaves the house, he will tail her. We will soon know if she has called in the cops.'

Ricardo glanced down at his wrist-watch.

'We leave in one hour. Get some rest.'

'I will,' said Miguel.

'Not *you*, stupid! I was talking to Faulkner.'

Even though he was caught up in his own terrible crisis, the American still showed concern for others.

'What about those kids?'

'Forget 'em,' advised Ricardo.

'Do they come with us?'

'No.'

'You can't *leave* them on that island,' he protested.

'I can do whatever I like,' affirmed the other.

'I thought they were going to be hostages,' said Miguel.

'Only if needed.'

'And if they're not?'

'Too bad. They can stay where they are.'

'That's murder!' argued Faulkner.

'It's what happens to people who cross me,' warned Ricardo, levelly. 'Put those kids out of your mind. You have enough to worry about. Just you pray that your wife follows my instructions.' He came to stand right over the American. 'Otherwise, you got problems.'

Helen Faulkner was a slim, handsome woman with a reputation for being an excellent hostess and an immaculate dresser. The last few days had transformed her. Fear had etched deep lines in her face and she just moped around the house in her old slacks and blouse. Ricardo's voice had convinced her that he meant business. She would co-operate.

She let herself into her husband's study and looked around. It was a large, high, scrupulously tidy room with luxurious furniture and fittings. It said everything about her husband's personality.

Helen kept tears at bay and crossed to the desk. She put down the black briefcase she was carrying, then unlocked a door. In a secret compartment at the rear of it was a slip of paper. She took it to the wall-safe and read the combination off it.

The tumblers clicked into place and the heavy door swung open. She felt a pang of remorse when she looked at what was inside. But she had no alternative. To save her husband, she had to do what they had told her and that meant incurring a great loss.

She filled the briefcase then flicked the catches back into position. Apprehension grew as she realised the value of what she was holding in her hand.

Then she recalled the menacing tone of the Cuban.

Five minutes later, she slipped out of the house and got into her car. As it turned out of the drive, a van followed it from a discreet distance.

Luis was trailing her carefully.

Thinking about what was in her briefcase.

Further attempts to batter their way out had left Nick and Jenny even more dejected. They groped around for what comfort they could find. Their hopes, as usual, were pinned on Max.

'Daddy will find us,' announced Jenny.

'Yes. When he realises we're missing, he'll search every Key in the Gulf of Mexico. We simply have to be patient.'

'Only trouble is that those men will be far away by then. They'll have collected their ransom and made their getaway.'

'Mr Faulkner must be rich.'

'Very rich. Otherwise, they wouldn't take all these risks.'

'They're such horrible men!'

'I know.'

'We *can't* let them win, Nick.'

'What can we do about it while we're locked in here?'

Jenny paced up and down the cabin like a caged animal.

'I'll go mad if we have to stay here much longer.' She flung herself at the door again and beat it with her fists. 'Help!!!!'

'There's nobody out there, Jenny.'

But she continued to make a resounding clamour.

'We're down here! Help!!! Under the ground!'

The cabin became an echo chamber as she pummelled away and Nick covered his ears against the din. Eventually, she gave up and slumped into a chair. She was confident that her father would come in search of them but she was not at all sure that he would trace them to the hideout.

They were entombed. Perhaps for ever.

'Nick...'

'Be quiet!'

'I only wanted to say that ——'

'Listen!' he interrupted. 'Thought I heard something.'

It was a faint rustling from up above. Jenny needed no more encouragement. She renewed her assault on the door and yelled even louder this time. Nick joined in.

'Help!!!!'

'There's an entrance behind the bushes!'

'Come down the ladder!'

'Here we are! Get us out!'

They almost swooned with relief when they heard an answering bang on the outside of the door. It was followed by a rhythmical thumping that made them step right back. The log which had helped to reinforce the door was now being used as a battering ram against it. The force of the pounding soon had its effect.

With a loud crack, the lock gave and the door swung open.

Their joy turned to bewilderment.

It was Ed Garrett.

Ernest was perched as ever on his cap.

'Give us a kiss,' he squawked.

Captain Valdano ducked beneath the swishing blade then reached for a chair with which to defend himself. As Redbeard came at him again, he parried the cutlass with the legs of the chair and then threw it violently into the pirate's midriff. Redbeard gasped for air and Valdano leapt in.

Wrenching the weapon from his enemy's grasp, he kicked the man to the deck and stood over him. The point of the cutlass was at the giant's throat. He had been beaten.

The Phantom Pirate was invincible.

Glad that another day's shooting was over, Max rushed to the boat that would take them back to the *Florida Queen*. Redbeard sat beside him. Pete Rudge, the mammoth Yorkshireman who played the part, had a message for his boss. In the film, they were mortal foes but the men were close friends in reality.

'No sign of them yet, Max?' asked Pete.

'Afraid not.'

'Fiona says your lass might've been after buried treasure.'

'I wish I knew, Pete.'

'Happen they'll be back before long.'

'I hope so.'

'If they're not,' added the huge stunt man, 'you'll want to go and search for them, I daresay.'

'Of course.'

'Count me in. And the rest of the team. We're all in this.'

Max was deeply touched.

'Thanks, Pete.'

He knew that he would need all the help he could get.

'However did you track us down?' said Jenny, still shaking with relief.

'I figured you'd come back here somehow,' explained Ed, plucking at his grizzled beard. 'You'd told me which Key it was in the group so I decided to sail over and take a look.'

'Hoist the mainsail!' suggested Ernest.

'*He* insisted on coming along for the trip as well.'

The children were both pleased to see the parrot.

'Lower a longboat!'

'Ignore him,' advised Ed.

He looked from Nick to Jenny and then back again. Deeply grateful as they were, he could detect something else in their gaze as well. A hint of suspicion. It was time to be honest with them.

'I owe you guys an apology,' he volunteered.

'What for?' said Jenny.

'Thing is, I did something real bad when I took on this job.'

'Bad?' Nick was watching him carefully.

'Didn't realise it at the time, mind you. But that's no excuse.'

'What happened?' asked Jenny.

'I'll tell you.' He grimaced slightly then plunged into his tale. 'You've heard me talk about Captain Tony's Saloon on Greene Street. In the old days, it went by the name of Sloppy Joe's.'

'Wasn't that Hemingway's favourite bar?' said Nick.

'You've got it.'

'Set 'em up, Joe!' shrieked Ernest. 'The drinks are on me!'

'Anyway,' continued Ed, 'I'm sitting in there one day when in comes this tall Cuban guy with shades on. Real friendly, he was. Bought me a drink and asked me if I'd like to earn five hundred bucks. So I told him I would.'

'What did you have to do for the money?' said Jenny.

'That was the catch. He knew I was working on this film, see, and that I'd advise on the best location. For five hundred dollars, I was to keep people well away from these Keys. That's why I told you to sail due west for your bird-watching even though I knew you'd see just as many species up here. Way *I* saw it, I wasn't really doing any harm. I had no idea what the Cuban gentleman was really up to. He could have been diving round here or had some other perfectly good reason not to want any interruptions.'

'Instead of which, he was a kidnapper,' observed Nick.

'I know that now. At the time, never crossed my mind.'

'We thought you were in on it,' admitted Jenny.

'Don't blame you. In a way, I was, though I was too blind to see it. That trouble up in the Everglades made me think. For a lousy five hundred bucks, I was putting good friends like you two in danger. That did it. I stashed the money in my pocket and came down here to give it straight back. I want no more of this crummy deal.'

'Shiver me timbers!' remarked Ernest.

'Something smelled fishy,' resumed Ed. 'So I boxed clever. Instead of sailing right here from the harbour, I went in a semicircle and hit this group from the north-west. I figured they'd see me coming the other way so I chose the back door.'

'Thank goodness you did!' noted Jenny.

'Did you see our boat over on the next island?'

'Yeah,' returned Ed. 'I knew at once you'd gotten yourselves into trouble. I sneaked ashore here and poked around. You know the rest.'

Their faith in him was restored. Not only had he rescued them from a dreadful fate, he had been very frank about his mistake and obviously wanted to set things right.

'I came to hand some dough back,' he said, wryly, 'and I find myself in the middle of a kidnap. Who's the target?'

'Ever heard of a man called Faulkner?' said Nick.

Ed chuckled. '*Heard* of him? Brad Faulkner is one of the richest guys in Florida. Big shipping magnate. Always spreading his money round for charity.'

'What sort of ransom could they ask for him?' said Jenny.

'Couldn't put a price on it,' replied Ed. 'But we gotta be talking in millions. That Faulkner is one wealthy son-of-a-gun.'

'We've got to save him,' insisted Nick.

'Sure. But how?'

'Find out when they're collecting their ransom and tell the police,' suggested Jenny. 'And I know just how to get the information.'

'How?'

'By overhearing it. I bet they're talking about it right now. All we have to do is to sneak over there and listen in.'

'We'd never get over there unnoticed,' argued Nick. 'The motor on Ed's dinghy would be a dead giveaway.'

'That's why *I'm* the person to handle this,' she

declared.

'You?'

'I'm the best swimmer.'

Ed Garrett and Nick were both dumbfounded. Jenny would be taking an enormous risk.

Helen Faulkner wished that she could drive faster but it was such a long time since she had been behind the wheel of a car and her confidence was not what it should have been. Having a chauffeur to take her everywhere had made her lose her touch as a driver. And it was so essential that she did the drive in the way instructed.

She checked her mirror. The van was still on her tail. She knew it was one of them and the fact only made her more uneasy. Yet another bridge loomed up ahead and she was soon cruising over it on her way to the next Key in the chain.

The briefcase lay on the back seat.

Helen knew that the ransom was an appallingly high price to pay but she wanted her husband back. In one piece.

Nothing else mattered, really.

Jenny used a strong, economical breastroke to take herself through the water. The other island was about half a mile away from theirs and it took some time to get there. Fearing that she might be spotted, she stayed underwater for a lot of the way. It was only when she got there that she realised how difficult a task she had set herself.

But she was not abashed. The two Cubans had left Jenny and her brother in the most awful predicament. She wanted revenge.

Jenny stayed low and headed for the sound of voices.

Ricardo was explaining it all to Miguel.

'The drop will be made at Big Pine.'

'Why?'

'Because that's where we have the yacht waiting. Don't you remember *anything,* Miguel?'

'Sorry.' He brightened. 'When do we have the share-out.'

'When I say.'

'Luis and me want our cut soon.'

'You'll get it. Minus a certain amount.'

'Minus!'

'For bungling. Luis let that kid escape him at the Everglades and you let a slip of a girl knock you out with a spade.'

Miguel's head began to throb once more.

Jenny had heard enough to pass on the vital information. The stunt world now proved its value. During an earlier holiday, when Max was working on a film about the Royal Navy, she had picked up the basics of semaphore. She now used what she had learned to send the message back to the other island. Ed would decode her message.

Big Pine. Another Key in the main string.

If anything happened to her, at least the

others would know what she had found out. Flushed by her success as a spy, she decided to try a little sabotage. If she could somehow steal or disable the launch and the boat, then the Cubans would be stranded on the island with Faulkner. The police could simply be told to come out and arrest them. The thought pleased her.

Still dripping, she scampered across the beach and hopped into the launch. Her hope had been that she would find the ignition key in place so that she could start up the engine, surge off across the water and drag the boat from the *Florida Star* behind her.

But the ignition key was not there.

Voices were on the move. Panic made her dive under a tarpaulin. She crossed her fingers that they would not find her. Jenny felt the launch bob three times as someone came aboard.

The engine was switched on and let out a deep-throated roar. Ricardo got Miguel to haul in the anchor then he took the launch off at speed. Jenny went with it.

Unwittingly, she was a stowaway.

She knew there would be no sympathy if she were caught.

Eight

Seabird

Nick and Ed Garrett had witnessed it all through their binoculars and they feared for Jenny's safety. Her daring had put her in hazard. They remained out of sight behind some trees as the launch thundered past on its way to the rendezvous at Big Pine. The boat from the *Florida Star* had now been cut adrift and was floating aimlessly near the other island. Ricardo and Miguel were in too big a hurry to want the trouble of towing it along.

The friends stepped out from their hiding place.

'Let's go after them!' urged Nick.

'Not so fast, old buddy,' warned the other.

'But they're getting away.'

'Precious little we can do about it at the moment, Nick. A dinghy with an outboard motor is no match for that launch. Besides, if we give chase too soon, they'll see us.'

'That's a point.'

'We'll catch up with them somehow, don't worry.'

Ed Garrett led the way to the other side of the island where he had moored his own craft. Ernest hopped off his head and took up a position on the prow.

'Whale ahead! Thar she blows!'

Nick helped the old man to run the dinghy back into the water then they both scrambled in. When the launch was a considerable distance away, the outboard motor was started up. They chugged out past the colony of frigate birds and gave chase.

'Why ever did Jenny climb aboard like that?' said Nick.

'It's called adventure.'

'Those men are quite unscrupulous.'

'Let's hope they don't find her.'

'They're bound to!'

'How good is she at playing possum?'

'Jenny can't lie still for two minutes.'

'First things first,' decided Ed. 'We must get word to your father. He's probably sick with worry over you two.'

'We should have been more honest with him about all this.'

'Too late to say that now, Nick.'

'Dad will want to go straight after Jenny. No holding back.'

'We'll see,' said Ed. 'When we get back to the yacht, we can send word to the cops. They should be in on this. Kidnapping is big business. They take it very seriously.'

'Why Mr Faulkner?'

'What?'

'Why was he the target? Because he's so wealthy?'

'That's one reason. Another may be political.'

'Political?'

'Those two guys are Cubans,' explained Ed. 'As you know, the United States and Cuba don't exactly see eye to eye. We believe in democracy and they prefer communism. The Cubans claim to love their country and yet they leave it by the boat-load to come here. It's a major problem in Florida.'

'What is?'

'Illegal immigrants. They sneak in all over the place. You simply can't patrol the whole coast-line.'

'Where does Mr Faulkner fit into all this?'

'He found out that one of his own ships was being used to bring a consignment of Cubans into the country. Don't ask me how, but they'd gotten two hundred guys on board. No American passports, no work permits, no nothing.'

'What did he do?' asked Nick.

'Blew the whistle on 'em. As soon as the ship docked, immigration officials swarmed over it. Every Cuban aboard was shipped back to Havana on the next boat.' He gave an elaborate shrug. 'Okay, you can say the man was only doing his patriotic duty in reporting those guys but it sure didn't make him too popular among Cubans.'

'And you think the kidnap is linked up with that?'

'I got a hunch, that's all.'

The motor launch was maintaining a much faster speed than they could muster and it was almost out of sight. Ed opened the throttle to get maximum thrust from the motor.

Nick admired the casual ease with which the sailor handled the dinghy. It was comforting to be sailing with a true veteran. He knew he had regained a friend.

Max Rawson pored over the map and used his pencils to draw circles around clusters of islands. All members of the stunt team - Liza Davies included - had insisted on joining in the search. Everyone got on well with the children and they wanted to find them as soon as conceivably possible. Max divided them up into groups and gave them all their orders.

'What about us?' wondered Liza.

'We'll sail due north,' he said. 'That's the likeliest area.'

'Let's go.'

'The response has been amazing. I can't thank you all enough.'

'Don't try,' counselled Pete Rudge. 'Let's just find those kids.'

'Lead the way!' ordered Max.

He and Liza were soon climbing into a small motor boat. All kinds of craft had been pressed into service for the search. The flotilla went out past the sailing ship then broke up and scattered.

Max set his course and went full speed ahead.

He was in a tense mood and started talking to himself.

'Buried treasure, indeed! *I'll* give them buried treasure.'

'Don't be too harsh on them, Max.'

'Look at all the bother they've caused.'

'There's probably a very simple explanation for it.'

'Yes,' he retorted. 'They didn't take the trouble to let their own father in on the secret of where they were going.'

'Give them the benefit of the doubt.'

About to reply, he took a deep breath instead. 'I'll try.'

Max steered while Liza acted as lookout. Her binoculars at last came into their own. She used a hand to point.

'Small craft coming this way.'

'Is it them? Is it Nick and Jenny?'

'I can't see properly...'

She kept the glasses trained on the dinghy until it got a little closer. The figure of Ed Garrett was clearly recongisable now and she was fairly sure that Nick was with him.

'What about Jenny?' asked the anxious Max.

'I don't see her at the moment.'

'But she went with Nick. She must be coming back with him.'

'Not this time. There are only three persons on board that craft. Ed, Nick and Ernest. No sign of Jenny.'

'There must be. Give me the glasses.'

But he saw exactly the same as Liza.

A man, a boy and a parrot.

Where on earth was Jenny?

Pleasure at seeing his son was quickly offset by anxiety about his daughter. Max made the motor boat positively skim the water.

He was in a hurry to get an answer.

The launch was now well to the north-east of the *Florida Star* and making steady progress towards its destination. Faulkner had recovered even more during the trip and it encouraged the Cubans to goad him. He did his best to remain calm under their provocation.

'Why do you hate all Cubans?' pressed Ricardo.

'I don't.'

'What have we ever done to you?'

'What have *I* ever done to *you*?'

'Don't look so innocent, Faulkner,' sneered Miguel. 'We know what happened to that ship of yours. You betrayed our countrymen.'

'They were breaking the law.'

'Everyone does that now and then,' argued Ricardo. 'You know it only too well. No man gets as rich as you are by sticking to the rules. You make your own.'

Faulkner let them take him to task. His eye had fallen on the automatic pistol which was lying beside Ricardo. If he could grab it, there might yet be a chance to save himself. He mustered all his strength and waited for the moment. It came when Ricardo turned his head away to scan the horizon.

Hurling himself forward, the American made a grab for the gun. It was a forlorn gesture. His legs were far too unsteady and he was all but thrown off balance. Ricardo snatched up the weapon and prodded him in the chest with it.

'I don't like heroes,' he said. 'Sit down again.'

'I'll get even somehow.'

'Sit down!'

As he barked the command, the Cuban used his other hand to shove Faulkner away. He stumbled awkwardly and fell against the tarpaulin under which Jenny was still lying.

'Ahhhh!'

Her scream was involuntary. And quite fatal.

Miguel pounced on the tarpaulin and dragged it back. Jenny was caught. Faulkner was immediately apologetic.

'I do beg your pardon, young lady. I had no idea.'

'How did *you* get here?' demanded Ricardo.

'How did she escape from the hideaway?' asked Miguel. 'That's what I want to know. Houdini could not escape from there.'

'Leave the child alone,' defended Faulkner.

'This is none of your business,' warned Ricardo.

'Yes, it is. You kidnapped me and demanded a ransom. You may or may not get what you're after. But there's certainly no need to drag her into it.'

'She dragged herself into it,' rejoined Miguel.
'Let her go.'
'No.'
'But she's no use to you. *I'm* the person you want.'
'Be quiet!' yelled Ricardo, wielding his gun. 'And sit down! Both of you!'
'Do as he says,' advised Miguel. 'He has a short fuse.'
Faulkner sat down in the stern beside Jenny.
'Thank you for standing up for me,' she said.
'You're the one who deserves the thanks. You and your brother were saviours to me on that island. I'd never have pulled through without you.'
'I'm not afraid of them,' announced Jenny, bravely.
Ricardo gave her a long, cold, unnerving stare.
He was trying to work out exactly what to do with her.

Reunited with his father, Nick quickly supplied him with the details of their latest visit to the island. Max was shaken to learn that they had exposed themselves to danger so readily and the news that Jenny was hiding aboard the Cuban craft was even more disturbing.
The motor boat made an arc in the water then headed back for the *Florida Star*. At the wheel, Max Rawson was thinking hard.
'Ed says we should call the police, Dad.'

‘We will. From the yacht.’
‘Jenny just had bad luck, that’s all.’
‘Sounds to me as if she asked for it,’ he observed, ruefully. ‘If you walk into trouble like that, you find it in large doses.’
Nick hung his head. Since he was slightly older than his sister, he felt responsible for her. While he was safe and sound, she was in the clutches of two vicious criminals.
‘Big Pine, you say?’ asked Max.
‘Yes.’
‘That’s not too far away,’ noted Liza.
‘I think we might go up there, Liza,’ said Max. ‘In style.’
‘What do you mean, Dad?’
‘Oh, you won’t be left out, Nick, have no fear. We’ll need everybody.
‘Including me?’ wondered Liza.
‘Especially you.’
Neither she nor Nick was any the wiser.
Max had a plan that had brought a little smile back to his face.
They knew that it was a good one.

Helen Faulkner sat on the almost deserted quay at Big Pine and surveyed the boats in the harbour. In the fading light of the late evening, they had an aura of romance about them but it was one that she did not notice. Her mind was concentrating on one thing only.
Getting her husband back again.
She was not alone. When she glanced in her

wing mirror, she could see the van that had followed her. It was parked behind her and a thickset young Cuban was at the driving wheel.

The wait was an agony. Ultimately, it came to an end.

A launch was coming towards her over the shadowed sea and she thought she could make out the figure of her husband in the stern. The van flashed its lights twice by way of a signal and the launch came up to the quayside.

A tall Cuban with sunglasses soon appeared. He beckoned her.

Helen took the briefcase and stepped towards him with great trepidation. She stopped a yard from him and handed him the case. He opened it, took out a large buff envelope, then extracted something that made his eyes smoulder with joy.

'It's all here,' he agreed.

'Where's my husband?' she implored.

'You can have him back,' said Ricardo with contempt. He held up the envelope. '*This* is what I want. It's the best way to hurt him. That's why we chose it.'

He snapped his fingers and Miguel came up the stone steps with Faulkner. The American was still fatigued but he revived when he saw his wife. She ran to his arms and they embraced.

Suddenly, the whole quay was ablaze with light.

Police squad cars came speeding in and squealed to a halt. A searchlight was turned on the Cubans. An ambulance which appeared on the scene left its headlights dazzling away.

'It's a trap!' yelled Ricardo.

'No!' denied Helen.

'Run, Luis.'

The thickset Cuban took the advice at once. Jumping out of his van, he eluded a couple of policemen and raced to the quayside. Uniformed officers moved forwards but their advance was soon checked.

Ricardo had gone to fetch Jenny. His gun rested against her head.

'Back off or she gets it!' he warned.

The police stopped and waited for a signal from their superior.

'Back off!' screamed Ricardo.

'You heard the man,' called the lieutenant.

The police withdrew to their cars and the three Cubans backed towards the launch. Using Jenny as a shield, they went back down the steps and into the craft. It churned water fiercely as it swung away. Jenny was helpless. She now had three wild-eyed Cubans in the boat with her.

A hundred yards or so out, they transferred to a small yacht. The Cubans had it mobile within seconds and it glided its way out towards open sea. The men congratulated themselves.

They had got what they had come for and made their escape. Jenny Rawson was the crucial factor. As long as she was aboard, the police launches would not dare to attack. All that the Cubans had to do was to sail out of

American waters.

'Was everything in the envelope?' asked Miguel.

'Everything,' confirmed Ricardo. 'We're rich!'

Luis was ecstatic. 'Cuba – here we come!'

Their celebrations were then rudely curtailed.

Out of the semi-darkness came a sight that astounded them. It was the sailing ship from the film, fully-rigged and manned by a crew of stuntmen who were also experienced sailors. Ed Garrett was on the poop deck, shouting orders to those aloft. Nick was standing beside him. Liza Davies was up on the rigging. Pete Rudge was leaning over a bulwark.

And Max Rawson was up among the billowing sails somewhere.

'Now!' he bellowed.

Everything happened at once.

The tall ship swung in, perilously near to the yacht. Grappling irons were used to hold the two vessels together. Pete Rudge and Liza Davies stormed on to the yacht. With the fury of a Redbeard, Pete picked up Luis in a bear hug and squeezed until he begged for mercy. Before the other Cubans knew what was going on, Liza had grabbed hold of Jenny and hauled her out of their reach.

When Miguel pulled out his knife, he found himself enmeshed in a net that Nick and Ed threw over him. When Luis tried to fight back against Pete, the vengeful giant lifted him bodily in the air and flung him over the side into the sea.

Only Ricardo was left. Gun in hand, he held everyone off.

Then Max Rawson entered the fray from the air.

Swinging across on a rope, he caught Ricardo with both feet and knocked him flying. The gun slithered across the deck. As the tall Cuban got up again, Max was on him in a flash, fighting with the spirit of a father with a score to settle.

His first punch made Ricardo reel. The second one had him dizzy and the third one knocked him to the floor. He lay groaning on the deck, wondering what had hit him. Ed Garrett boarded the yacht and stood over the fallen Cuban.

'Here,' he said. 'Have this back.'

The twenty dollar bills floated down all over him

Jenny now ran to her father who embraced her warmly. Nick joined them to complete the family reunion.

'Are you okay, Jenny?' asked Max.

'Fine.'

'Did they hurt you?' said Nick.

'They wouldn't know how to,' she retorted.

'That's a brave girl you got there, Max,' noted Ed.

'I'll go along with that,' added Liza.

Jenny basked in the praise then looked at all

the friendly faces that now surrounded her. It is not every young girl who is rescued by the crew of the Phantom Pirate but she did not shower them with thanks at first. Jenny offered mild criticism.

'What kept you?'

The house had a stupendous view out over Miami beach and the visitors stood at the picture windows and gaped. Faulkner had insisted on inviting Max and his children to stay for a few days and they were delighted to accept. The opulence of their surroundings was overwhelming at first but Jenny quickly adjusted.

It *was* like being in an episode of *Miami Vice*.

Over drinks, Max raised a question which had baffled him.

'What was in that brown envelope?'

'Can't you guess?'

'I thought there'd be money in the briefcase,' said Nick.

'Or diamonds and rubies,' added Jenny.

'It was something rather more valuable.'

'Microfilm?' suggested Max. 'Nuclear secrets?'

'Nothing as sinister as that,' said the American with a chuckle.

'Show them, dear,' suggested his wife.

Faulkner crossed to a table and picked up the envelope. With the utmost reverence, he took out something and spread them out on the table. Max and the children crowded around.

Jenny was patently disappointed.

'Is that all? Stamps!'

'Rare stamps,' corrected Faulkner. 'My hobby. What you see here is worth millions. That was the attraction, you see. They're so easy to carry and to conceal. Far better than wads of notes or bars of gold bullion.'

'The collection has been my husband's life's work,' explained Helen Faulkner. 'It's been a labour of love.'

'And here's the pride of my collection,' he announced, taking a last sheet out of the envelope. 'What do you think of these, Nick?'

The boy recognised the birds at once.

'They're cormorants.'

'Where are the stamps from?' asked Jenny.

'Chile. Part of a limited issue at the end of the last century. Most of them were destroyed in a fire before they went on sale and only a few survived.' He waved a hand at the colourful stamps which showed a cormorant in flight above an azure sea. 'I have them all.'

'How much are they worth?' said Max.

'As much as all the others put together.'

'Wow!' Jenny was impressed. 'No wonder you didn't want to lose them.'

'Now you understand what I was muttering on the island.'

'Yes,' agreed Nick. 'I do.'

Seabird.

If you have enjoyed *Seabird*, you might like to read ACTION SCENE 1 – SKYDIVE:

ACTION SCENE 1
SKYDIVE

KEITH MILES

On location with their father, the film stuntman, Max Rawson, Nick and Jenny find themselves involved in some daring and dangerous action of their own. Caught up in a case of international espionage, they find themselves in the hands of two ruthless Welsh criminals, who seek to imprison them high in the Snowdonian mountains, with no chance of their being rescued.

But, when it comes to getting out of difficult situations, it isn't only Max Rawson who can perform the stunts...

KNIGHT BOOKS